Return to Victoria Island

by

Karen Andover

A Prequel to Sanctuary on Victoria Island

Cover Art by *Tina Lynn Stout*

The Wild Rose Press, Inc.
PO Box 708
Adams Basin, NY 14410-0708
Visit us at www.thewildrosepress.com

Publishing History
First Edition, 2025
Trade Paperback ISBN 978-1-5092-6012-6
Digital ISBN 978-1-5092-6013-3

Victoria Island Series
Published in the United States of America

Chapter 1

One month ago
Atlanta

Maggie "Ruthless" Ruth, an attractive woman in her mid-fifties who radiated *expensive good taste*, removed her reading glasses. She toyed with the arms of her spectacles before setting them down on her elegant French country desk. Standard lamps sat on an antique credenza behind her and cast a flattering glow on her complexion. A vase with white roses graced her desk. The office décor announced that the occupant "had arrived."

Anticipation shot through Ava like a bolt of lightning. Finally, her hard work had paid off. She had so many ideas to create efficiencies and improve the client experience. She couldn't wait to start.

Savoring the moment, she crossed one leg over the other and adjusted the hem of her knee-length crepe navy-blue skirt. The designer suit had cost a lot, but everyone said you had to dress for the job you wanted and not the one you had. She tucked a strand of long brown hair behind her ear and exposed her plain silver ball earrings. The decades-old accounting firm favored conservative attire.

"Speaking on behalf of everyone on the management team, we wanted you to know how much we value your dedication and achievements." Lines around Maggie's mouth creased as she pursed her lips. "Having said that"—she peeked at her watch before she continued—"unfortunately, we don't think you're the best qualified candidate for the job. And so, we wanted to let you know we have selected another candidate for the position."

What?

The butterflies in Ava's stomach dropped like an out-of-control roller coaster cresting the top and rushing down the hill. Coldness washed over her. She squeezed her eyes shut, hoping tears would not leak out. She squashed a memory of her high school guidance counselor frowning over her grade report and recommending she consider other careers instead of applying to college.

All those years of hard work. What had it all been for?

She stared blankly at the woman she had considered a mentor who had singlehandedly derailed her career ambitions in under thirty seconds.

Maggie arched an elegantly shaped eyebrow and drummed her French manicured fingers on the arms of her paisley-print upholstered chair. When the silence became overwhelming, Ava broke eye contact and glanced away. Her mind raced. How could this have happened? She had spent long hours at her desk ensuring she hit her performance targets. Her reviews had all been excellent. Her work product and client relations were superb. What went wrong?

Maggie's lips were moving but she didn't hear anything. She shook her head to clear her thoughts. *Focus.*

"We wanted to give you advance notice that we have selected Sheila Grosvenor for the position. We'll make the announcement at tomorrow's staff meeting," Maggie said.

Ava bit her lip. This is going from bad to worse. *Sheila? She's not a team player. She hasn't even been here as long as I have.* The silence stretched uncomfortably long and, finally, she cleared her throat.

"My work has been exemplary. Why wasn't I the best qualified among the candidates? I've been a team leader longer than Sheila and I have more experience. My clients have always been very happy with my work."

"I'm not disagreeing with you." Maggie straightened a pile of papers on her desk. "No one doubts your professional competence. Or your dedication. The Board felt that the position required someone who was able to bring in the big accounts. Sheila brought the Perfect Packaging business with her when she joined the firm. It's a large revenue maker for us. She has a higher profile among the corporate community than you do." She hesitated. "There is more to being the head of department than managing projects."

A pained look crossed Maggie's face. "Management must always set an example for employees. We have to be sensitive to exposure to harassment claims." Maggie folded her hands and rested them on the desk.

Toby. Ava's cheeks burned and she froze.

I guess we weren't as discreet as I thought.

Acid ate at her stomach. "I understand your decision," she said, cheeks heating. "I appreciate you letting me know in advance of the public announcement."

"You're welcome. As I said, we appreciate the work you have done here."

A fist slammed into Ava's midsection.

What does that mean?

Maggie cleared her throat. "The Board meets in two weeks." She moved her engraved gold pen so it was next to her buttery-soft leather diary. "These are difficult times. Only a lean business survives. And the Board of Directors wants to do more than that. They want the business to thrive. So about six months ago they engaged an outside consulting firm. Together with an in-house committee, they reviewed the corporate structure and have made suggestions to streamline the business. I chaired the committee, and I can tell you that if Penmans wants to succeed, we will have to adjust to shifts in demand. The recommendation to the Board is to rebalance the level of human capital. I support these findings and will be making a presentation to them to that effect. I believe the Board will accept them and make decisions with regard to retentions. Your client recruitment numbers have been unacceptably low. The company can't carry any dead weight."

"But I—"

Maggie held up her hand. "I'm afraid it's a harsh but true rule of the corporate world. You need to do good work, but you also need to grow the company. I suggest that if you want to keep your job, you recruit a high-value client in the next two weeks." She shook her head slowly. "Otherwise, I can't help you."

Her thoughts raced to her bank account. What

would she do if she lost her job? The large deposit on her townhome last year had significantly depleted her savings. She had chosen a home in an expensive area to maximize resale potential. It had seemed like a good idea at the time. She blanched. She couldn't run home to Mom and Dad. They would help her but at the cost of her self-respect. She couldn't be the child that never measured up to the standards her "golden child" older brother set.

With a slow nod, Ava got to her feet. She forced a smile. "I appreciate your candor. I better finish up a report that needs to go out tonight. Will you excuse me?" Her hand on the doorknob, she hesitated, before turning back toward Maggie. "I've got several weeks of accrued vacation time. I'd like to take it starting next week and focus on client development."

Maggie peeked over the top of her glasses. "If you think that is appropriate, then, yes, of course you may use your vacation time." She waved her off and turned to her computer.

Ava walked stiffly out of Maggie's office and held her head high. She passed Robert sitting at the receptionist's desk. His head was averted as he rummaged in his desk drawer. There were no secrets from administrative staff.

Chapter 2

Wendy gave her two thumbs up, her black fingernail polish and Goth appearance incongruous with the genteel office décor. "How did it go?"

Ava grimaced and shook her head. She couldn't force herself to vocalize the news. So much for taking Wendy with her. She was a highly intelligent and organized assistant but not everyone appreciated her sense of style. She hoped Wendy survived her fall from grace. New management always made personnel changes.

"I'll be in my office if you need me." She closed the office door behind her and slumped into her sleek black leather "low-level executive" chair. She had been hoping to upgrade her office furniture with the promotion. She rubbed her aching cheeks. No one's face had ever cracked from pasting on a fake smile. Or so she hoped.

"Damn. Damn. Damn." There was no chance of returning to the Gateway account this afternoon. She beat a staccato rhythm on her desk with her fingers. How on earth would she come up with a wealthy new client in under two weeks when she hadn't managed to do so in the past? Her client development had always been small to medium enterprises. She needed to go big or go home. Literally.

A short knock sounded on the door.

"Come in," Ava called out.

Wendy opened it and poked her head in. "Are you okay?" Skull and crossbones earrings dangled from her ears and matched her black lipstick.

Ava turned her attention to Wendy, her brow furrowed. "Is it all over the building already?"

"I'm afraid so." She pulled a face. "Sheila's assistant has been spreading the news down in the coffee shop."

"Ugh." Ava rolled her eyes. "Well, I guess it had to come out." She gave a slight shrug. That was how the business world worked. "The sooner I face it the better."

Ava's desk phone rang. "I'd better get this," Ava said.

"Of course." Wendy backed out of her office and closed the door quietly. Ava picked up the receiver.

"Hello, Ava," Toby said.

"Hi, Toby." She swallowed the lump in her throat.

"I'm glad I caught you before you left the office. I'm afraid…" Toby stumbled over his words. "Uh, I have to cancel our plans for tonight. I'm going to have to work late."

Ava slumped in her chair. "Oh. I understand." And she did. Toby had figured out she wasn't going to help him climb the career ladder. She choked back a bitter laugh. *Too bad I didn't figure it out earlier.*

The band of tension tightened around her head. "It's not a problem. Perhaps some other time."

Toby was quiet for a moment. "Sure, I'll get back to you on that. We'll talk later."

"Bye," Ava said, but Toby had already hung up.

Chapter 3

Victoria Island

Towering anvil-shaped gray clouds and gusty winds blew in from the Atlantic Ocean. Violent ocean swells hid rogue waves that threatened any ship unlucky to be in their path. A band of heavy rain sat like an ominous curtain on the horizon.

Jack Rutledge spun in his office chair and flung a glass paperweight against the wall. The impact fractured it, and pieces scattered around the floor. He scrubbed a hand over his face. The company account balances were lower than he had expected. Nothing too drastic or obvious. *Someone knew what they were doing.*

He clenched his fists. *Rutledge Properties was his creation.* It was a business that not only he, his brother, and sister depended on for income, but also many long-time employees whom he considered friends. But he had to face the truth. Someone was embezzling from *his* company. He swallowed the acid that rose in his throat. He knew every employee and every aspect of the business. Slamming his fist on the pedestal desk, he toppled a small replica of his first building project.

"Damn it." He restored the sculpture to its position.

Swiveling his chair, he gazed out the large picture window. Ocean waves crashed violently as the sky darkened in anticipation of a storm. He hadn't been this angry since he had found his fiancée in bed with one of his college friends. A picture blazed in his head of Janice naked and writhing underneath his fraternity brother, Billy Lesser.

He choked off the memory that was forever burned in his mind and forced himself to return his focus to the impending disaster facing his company. Self-recrimination over the theft was useless. He would deal with the issue once the employee was identified. The priority had to be to stop the bleeding. It was problematic to call in a local accounting firm. Gossip about the embezzlement would hurt his business reputation. What could he do? He needed a discreet solution.

His cell phone vibrated. Glancing at the name on the screen, he hit the answer button. "Hi, George. Good to hear from you." He cringed at his monotone which would signal a problem to his construction foreman. Forcing interest into his voice, he continued, "I didn't realize you were back in town yet."

"Good morning, Jack. We just got back yesterday."

Because it would be expected, he asked, "How was your week off?"

"Good. Marie and I took the kids to my in-laws' cabin by the lake. I had the best of both worlds. My in-laws watched the kids and Marie and I had some quality time together."

"Sounds like a great vacation but it's good to have you back." He hoped his enthusiasm sounded sincere. "I'm concerned about the medical center project. It's behind schedule."

George cleared his throat. "That's why I'm calling.

Jim called this morning and said he had to push back the concrete delivery until next week. Staffing problems or something. Some damn summer cold going around."

"Shit." He thought about the tight subcontractor timetables. Any delay would cause problems down the supply chain. "That's going to make the schedule even tighter. We won't have any wiggle room for any more screw-ups, or we'll have to pay contract penalties."

"I know, boss. I'm on it. I made it clear that if Jim wants any more business from Rutledge, then he had better make sure that there are no more delays. He said he would have the concrete trucks out next week if he had to drive them one-by-one himself."

Jack let out a reluctant laugh. "And he would, too. Jim and I have worked together for a long time. He's always come through for me." He gave a long exhale. "I guess there is nothing we can do about that. Can you repurpose the workers so we don't lose any other time on the project?"

"As it happens, they were behind on installing the plumbing pipes. I've given them a good swift kick up the ass. They'll work on that tomorrow."

Jack swore. "So we couldn't have poured the concrete anyway, is that what you're telling me?"

George coughed. "Yeah, that about sums it up."

He clenched his cell phone so hard his knuckles turned white. "All right. I trust you'll get this shitshow back on track."

George was quiet for a moment. "I will, boss."

Jack ended the call.

When it rained, it poured. Right now, it was a fuckin' monsoon.

He glanced at his black diver's watch, a gift from

his father. *Late.* He powered down the computer. *They won't hold the game start for me.* He laughed mirthlessly. Grabbing his keys from the entryway table, he headed out the door. He hoped his mood would improve.

Chapter 4

Glass in hand, Ava plucked the chilled bottle of Italian prosecco from the refrigerator and bumped the appliance door shut with her hip. Instead of the off-the-shoulder blouse and palazzo pants she had planned to wear to the art gallery, she wore yoga pants and an oversized T-shirt. Her hair was in a messy bun.

So much for a celebratory drink with Toby. She tamped down that thought and poured some fizzy wine into a glass. Grimacing, she gazed thoughtfully at the bottle and then poured even more out. There was no point saving it.

Gulping some wine, she viewed her pristine open-plan home. A classic elegant white sofa and two side chairs made an inviting conversation area. A glass sculpture of an ocean wave sat on the granite-topped coffee table. Framed pen and ink drawings of marsh birds hung on the wall. The minimal décor was tasteful but devoid of color or personality. She looked around. Her home was cold and empty. Like her life.

Opening a kitchen drawer, she grabbed a pen and notepad. She put the items on a tray with the wine bottle and her glass and carried everything into the living area. Setting it down on the coffee table, she curled up on the sofa. She flipped the notebook open and scribbled two column headings. Pros and cons of working for Penmans. She contemplated the positives.

Safe employment. Interesting work. Good salary. Prestige. On the con side she listed several factors. Long hours. Client development requirements. Lack of employee morale. The phone rang, and she glanced at the screen. Her mother. Might as well get this over with.

She sat up tall and forced some cheerfulness into her voice. "Hi, Mom."

"Hi, Ava." Her mom sounded like an aging cheerleader. Ava could picture her in her signature twin sweater set and skirt with a string of pearls around her neck. Her glossy brown hair cut in a razor-sharp bob. "So today was the big day. Any news?"

"Well, yes, Mom. Unfortunately, just not the news I was hoping for."

Lilian made a sympathetic noise. "What do you mean, darling?"

"I didn't get the job," she stated flatly.

"I'm so sorry, darlin'." Lilian's elegant southern accent became more pronounced when she became emotional. "I know how hard you've been working for that promotion."

"Yes, well, things don't always go as planned." Ava twisted a long piece of hair that had come loose from her bun around her finger.

"That's my girl. There will be another opportunity for you. Something better will come along."

Ava pinched the bridge of her nose. Her mother could trot out any number of platitudes when needed. It was one of her best features, but it could also be her worst.

"Your father and I are so proud of you. You've accomplished so much in your career."

"Thanks, Mom. I'm trying to be philosophical about it. It wasn't meant to be. Or at least, not at this moment in time." She swallowed. "But to be honest, it's not easy. And I'm sure there is going to be lots of office gossip tomorrow." The swirling in her stomach intensified. She wandered back into the kitchen, opened a drawer, and rummaged around until she found the bottle of antacid tablets. Twisting the cap off, she tipped out a tablet and popped it in her mouth before defiantly taking another swallow of her prosecco and slamming the glass down. Stifling a curse, she grabbed a towel to mop up the spilled wine. "And that's not all. My boss basically said I need to get a good client before the next Board meeting in two weeks or I will be let go. Penmans is restructuring and I won't make the retention list unless I show I can be a rainmaker. I've arranged some vacation time with my supervisor." Her laugh lacked any real humor. "Frankly, I think she's happy to have me out of the office for a few weeks. I suspect she thinks the transition will go more smoothly if I'm not around. And I need free time if I'm going to land a prestigious client." Her voice cracked. "I'm not sure what to do."

Lillian's voice gentled. "I'm so sorry, Ava. You've done good work. You deserved the promotion. I know how hard you've worked to get to where you are."

Ava sniffed. *Please don't compare me to Nate.*

"Honey, large corporations can be cutthroat. You know your father started his career at a big law firm. He was much happier when he left."

Her father was a prominent tax attorney in the Atlanta area. For as long as Ava could remember, he had had his own firm. "I didn't realize that. Why did he leave?"

"Nate was four and you had just been born. He missed so much of Nate's early childhood. He wanted to be present for you both. He didn't want either of you growing up without knowing him. You know how demanding those large firms can be with their outrageous billing requirements. Those horror stories are all true. Leaving to start his own firm and work from home was the best thing he could have done. He didn't have to worry about leaving the office in time to put you to bed." She paused. "Of course, you know your father. He is such a hard worker and before long he was expanding and taking on a partner and associates. But at least as a founding partner, he had a lot more control over his schedule."

"I hadn't realized that." Ava's face softened. "I just remember Dad being around for our after-school activities."

Lillian cleared her throat. "The annual boat show at Victoria Island is next week. Your father always gets invitations to the events. Why don't you go and see if you can persuade some of those high rollers to move their business to Penmans? You can stay at the condo. It's not rented out at the moment."

Ava thought about her parents' holiday home on the barrier island off the northeast coast of Florida, a four-hundred-mile journey from Atlanta. Her happy place.

Tears welled up.

"Thanks, Mom. I appreciate it. That's as good an idea as any." She wiped the wetness on her cheeks with the back of her hand. "It's just been a really difficult day."

"I know, dear." Concern flooded her voice. "It's going to be hard to sign a new client in just two weeks. Your father spends months and even years on it. He always says client development is like a slow romance."

"I know, Mom," she whispered, "but I have to try."

"Of course you do, darling. I understand. Try to enjoy yourself even if it is a working holiday. Your father and I have always said you work too hard. You deserve a vacation." Lillian hesitated. "As it happens maybe you could help us out with something."

She sniffled. "Of course, Mom. You know I'll do anything I can to help. What's the problem?"

"Darling, your dad had a message from the property management company. We've had some negative reviews posted online, and the rental occupancy rate has been down this summer. It seems very odd. Anyway, the property manager wanted to talk to your father, but he's so busy preparing for an upcoming trial. I hate for him to be bothered with this. And you know you are so much better at resolving problems than I am. Can you find out what he wants?"

"I'd be happy to see what's going on with the condo. I can take care of contacting the property manager for you, Mom. Don't worry about that at all."

"Your father and I would very much appreciate it. And, darling, please don't be too dejected. There's always another job." Her mother was quiet for a moment. "How was the new art exhibit?"

The moment she had been dreading. How should she spin this for her mother? Should she try to manage the narrative or just be honest? *Maybe it's a good day to bury bad news.* Yes, that was definitely the strategy to take. It worked for politicians so it should work for her.

"We didn't go. Toby cancelled. He had to work late." The less said the better.

"Oh, it really hasn't been a great day for you, darling, has it?"

Ava's chest squeezed at her mother's words.

"When will you leave?"

"I think I'll leave early Saturday morning."

"All right. We'll talk soon. Love you."

"And you, Mom. Give my best to Dad."

Ava ended the call and set her cell phone on the coffee table next to the note pad. Enough wallowing. Time to put her plan into action. After swallowing the remains of the wine, she tipped another generous amount into her glass. She went into the bedroom and set the glass of prosecco down on the nightstand. Taking her suitcase out of the closet, she opened it on the bed. Her business suits hung in the front of the closet. She pushed them aside and reached into the back of the closet where her seldom-worn leisure clothes were. She flipped through the hangers, searching for clothes she would need for her impromptu trip. She pulled out several sundresses and laid them on the bed. She yanked out a few pairs of shorts and matching tops and threw them down. She grabbed her favorite little black dress. Her movements became increasingly jerky and frantic. Rummaging on the floor of the closet, she searched for a pair of sandals. She tossed aside her work heels, not caring where they landed. When she found a pair of sandals, she threw her work shoes back in the closet and shut the door. She tugged open her dresser drawer and snatched several pairs of underwear and bras. She piled them with the other clothes.

Abruptly she sat down on the bed. The tears streaming down her face escalated into sobs. Crying uncontrollably, she rolled over and curled into the fetal position. Finally, her tears slowed. Sitting up, she grabbed some tissues from the nightstand and blotted her eyes. *This is really stupid. Blubbering over a missed job opportunity or a failed relationship is pointless.* What would her colleagues think if they knew she was sobbing? That would be so humiliating. She wadded up the wet tissues and threw them in the trash. She gave a final wipe to her face with the backs of her hands.

Enough feeling sorry for myself.

Mechanically she folded her clothes and put them in the suitcase before closing it and moving it to the floor. She sniffed.

A difficult day required body armor.

She pulled her favorite pant suit out of the closet. She added a red blouse and high heeled pumps. She would dress to kill.

She shot a quick text to an old friend, letting her know she would be visiting the island.

Time for bed. Tomorrow would be difficult enough without looking like she hadn't slept. The best defense is a strong offense. Go big or go home. She stamped down a semi-hysterical laugh.

She was turning into her mother.

Chapter 5

Ava inched her car forward past orange
construction cones and merged into the long line of
traffic on the two-lane highway that led to Victoria
Island. The monotonous drive had given her ample time
to replay yesterday's misery in her head. As soon as she
had arrived in the office, she had sent Sheila a
congratulatory message. She had followed that with a
general e-mail inviting everyone to enjoy the donuts she
had left in the breakroom in honor of Sheila's
promotion. But the day had still been awkward.
Longtime colleagues had scattered like roaches as she
walked down the hallway.

The staff meeting at ten, when Sheila's promotion
had been officially announced, had been excruciating.
By the end of the conference, a jackhammer was
pounding in her head. It had been a very long day, and
now, on Saturday morning, she had a death grip on the
steering wheel. It had already been a tedious journey
from Atlanta. The tension in her shoulders radiated up
her neck and to the back of her head. She moved her
head from side to side to try and loosen the muscles in
her neck. It seemed everyone wanted to get out of the
city this weekend to enjoy the best of the early summer
weather. She tapped her fingers on the steering wheel,
silently fuming at the stalled traffic.

Stay calm. The worst of the congestion is behind

me.

Her spirits lifted and her tension eased with each mile that she got closer to the island.

Finally, she reached the intracoastal bridge and crossed onto the island.

Hello, Victoria Island. Goodbye, stress.

She lowered the window and a blast of hot, humid air hit her in the face. The rank stench of the marshland wafted through the open window. The pungent yet familiar smell was somehow comforting. A large osprey soared overhead, periodically diving closer to the water to hunt for fish.

Victoria Island was home to an historic town in the center north of the island and also boasted several large hotels which supported a healthy year-round tourist trade. In the winter, snowbirds from the north flocked to the island in search of warmer weather. In the summer, tourists from the southeast came to enjoy the beach. The center street downtown was filled with small independent shops selling everything a beach tourist could want, from tacky shell souvenirs to antiques and resort wear. The numerous restaurants, ice cream parlors, and coffee shops offered lots of opportunities to sit and relax. Picturesque homes built in the late 1800s surrounded the downtown area.

Several large resort hotels and communities dominated the south end of the island. The Beaches was a popular neighborhood anchored by a large oceanfront hotel with conference facilities, tennis courts, multiple swimming pools, and several restaurants. The adjacent housing community spread across the width of the island from the beach side with access to the Atlantic Ocean to the marsh side on the intracoastal waterway separating the island from the mainland. The gated neighborhood shared many amenities with the hotel, including a security force.

Ava flipped her turn signal on and turned right onto the island parkway. The arterial road leading to the south end of the island was covered by a canopy of water oak trees. Clumps of Spanish moss hung from the tree limbs overhanging the road.

Slowing, she exited the traffic circle and pulled up to the security gates. A quick press of her community card against the sensor and the gate lifted. Huge ancient oak canopy trees shaded the road. She drove along the winding roads, passing walkers and cyclists enjoying the neighborhood. She parked in front of her parents' townhome-style condominium.

Retrieving the key from the lockbox, she opened the door. The lemon scent of cleaning fluids hung in the air as she stepped into the entryway. The terracotta tile floors shone. The gold-streaked white marble kitchen island and appliances sparkled. She made a mental note to let her mother know that the cleaning staff the property management company hired was doing a good job.

She put her suitcase in the second bedroom on the rack at the end of the double bed. A seagrass chair with a green cushion sat in one corner of the room. A white-washed rattan dresser with a glass top matched the dual nightstands. The bed had a fluffy blue comforter with several nautical-themed accent pillows. Her stomach growled. She would check around more carefully later, but right now she needed to pick up groceries. She grabbed her purse and headed to the front door. Her cell phone rang. Digging her phone out of her handbag, she hit the answer button.

"Ms. Morrison, this is Benny Chavez with Beachside Properties." The property agent spoke with a slight Spanish accent. "Your mother gave me your number. I'd like to talk to you about your property, if you have a minute?"

"Hello, Mr. Chavez. I'm so glad you called. My mother said there was some sort of problem. Can you tell me what's going on?"

"Yes, I'm afraid there have been a few minor issues. Well, not with the condo itself. But there have been a number of complaints about the renters. Security has made numerous callouts."

"What kind of trouble?" Ava frowned. "My parents rent it out frequently to weekend or weekly visitors, and the rental income makes it cost effective to own. I can assure you that they want the renters to have a good experience. And they also wouldn't want any problems with the neighbors or with the Condo Association. As you know, the Condo Association has lots of rules." She sighed heavily. "They say the bylaws are designed to maintain an upscale and pleasant living environment. Unfortunately, I think they just pit neighbor against neighbor. But since they can impose fines for residents who don't follow the rules, we want to make sure we comply."

"I understand." He chuckled. "Most of my clients want to avoid problems.. In fact, I've never met a property owner who liked their management association. Anyway, the issues have been mostly noise complaints." Benny Chavez hesitated. "The odd thing is that Security has been unable to verify that any of the grievances were valid. By the time Security turns up, there is no excessive noise. The immediate neighbors deny calling Security or that there was ever any problem."

Ava's brows drew together. "Who has been calling in the complaints?"

"It's apparently an unknown caller each time."

Ava huffed. "So, an anonymous caller makes a noise complaint but there is no actual proof of any noise problem, is that right?"

"That about sums up the situation. Security is threatening to impose a fine for nuisance callouts. And more significantly, the renters have been annoyed by Security turning up at their door at all hours of the day and night. Several guests have posted unflattering comments." He cleared his throat. "You know the power of reviews. Consequently, reservations for the unit have been down this summer."

"Great." Ava wrinkled her nose. "What can we do about it?"

"It's a tough situation. I'm going to meet with Security and see if I can smooth things over. Generally, the Security officers are good guys. I think they're just fed up with the useless calls. But they need to take some responsibility for not getting information about the complainants. At this point, there is no evidence of visitors making unreasonable noise; rather the evidence is of Security hassling the renters, which is negatively impacting on the number of bookings. I'm confident I can resolve this. I just wanted you to be aware of what was going on."

"My parents have noticed the lower number of bookings this summer compared to last summer." She chewed her bottom lip. "Ironically, the lower uptake in rentals is how I was able to book it for myself. But I guess that's neither here nor there. Thanks, Mr. Chavez. I appreciate your efforts. Please let me know how your meeting goes with Security."

"Of course. I'll update you after I meet with them."

"Uh—Do you think it would be helpful if I attended the meeting with you?"

"Thanks for the offer. However, I think it would be better if I approach them alone. I have a good working relationship with Security. But if I believe they would be more receptive to an owner, I'll be sure to let you know."

"Thanks again, Mr. Chavez. I appreciate everything you do to take care of our property."

"Of course. It's our pleasure to take care of your property. Uh, there is one more thing."

"Oh? What is that?"

"There was some minor vandalism. A couple of decorative planters in the entryway were destroyed. It was quite a mess. The neighbors complained about dirt everywhere. Unfortunately, the Condo Association sent in workers to clean it up and presented me with the bill. I purchased new ones. I'll be adding the cleanup fees and replacement costs to your monthly account."

"Do they know who did it?"

"No, sadly not. Security asked around but no one saw anything. Anyway, thanks for your time. I'll keep you posted."

"I'll be anxious to hear from you with an update."
Ava punched the end call button on her cell phone and locked the door. As she was walking out to her car, the door of the neighboring unit opened and a diminutive lady wearing a white tennis dress came out. Her short

white hair was a cap of riotous curls.

Blue eyes twinkled and her wide smile displayed pearlescent white teeth. A tennis racket protruded from her oversized macrame bag. Her fluffy hair bounced as she hurried down the sidewalk.

"Hello, dear." She waved. "I'm Sadie Peterson. I just moved in a few months ago."

Ava set down her cavernous handbag and clasped Sadie's outstretched hand. "Hello, Sadie, I'm Ava Morrison."

"Where are you from, dear?" Sadie put a hand up shading her eyes as she squinted into the bright sunshine.

"I'm from Atlanta. My family has owned this condo for several years."

"Oh, how nice." Sadie beamed. "We'll be neighbors. It's so nice to have a permanent resident rather than renters. I recently moved here from New Jersey. Are you staying long?"

"On this visit, I'll be here about two weeks," Ava replied.

"Is it just you?" Her neighbor peered around her almost as if she expected someone else to appear.

"Just me. I'm afraid I have to get going." She gestured toward Sadie's tennis racket. "It was very nice meeting you. Enjoy your game."

"Thank you, I will, dear." Sadie said. "We must get together soon. I'm sure I'll see you around." Sadie adjusted her bag on her shoulder and bounded down the sidewalk toward her small two-door red convertible. She hit the button on her car remote to unlock it, opened the driver door, and tossed her tennis racket onto the passenger seat. Tires squealing, Sadie peeled out of the parking lot. Bemused, Ava watched her zoom off down the road.

A white SUV emblazoned with reflective yellow side stripes and a magnetic "Security" sign on the side panel passed the speeding red car and pulled into the parking lot. The driver stopped in the parking space directly in front of her condo. A lanky young man, dressed in the security unit's uniform of Beaches-branded blue polo shirt, khaki shorts, and baseball cap, got out of the vehicle. His hair was cut short in a military "high and tight" style. Mirrored aviator sunglasses shielded his eyes from the midday sun. A radio and a pair of handcuffs dangled from his leather belt. He held one hand over the gun in its holster.

"Hello, ma'am." He whipped off his sunglasses with the other hand and gave her a piercing stare.

"Hello, Officer." Ava smothered a smile. He couldn't be more than twenty years old. "How can I help you?"

"I'm Officer Chad Thornley. Are you renting this unit?" He gestured to the building behind her.

"No. I own it. Or at least my parents do. I'm Ava Morrison." She peeked at her watch and then back at him. "I'm sorry, but I've got errands to run. Is there something I can do for you?"

Officer Thornley crossed his arms over his chest. "I just like to have a friendly word with everyone. This neighborhood prides itself on being quiet and peaceful. I like to make sure all our guests know the rules. For example, if your residence has a garage, you're required to park inside." He pointed to her car. "Is that your vehicle, ma'am?"

Sweat rolled down her face. A typical muggy

Florida day. She wiped her forehead with the back of her hand. Officer Thornley did not appear to be sweating at all. So not fair. She exhaled noisily. "Yes, it is." She gestured behind her. "But as you can see, ours doesn't have a garage, so that rule is irrelevant."

"Just an example, ma'am. You have a nice day now, you hear?" He touched the peak of his baseball cap and turned and got back into his vehicle.

Ava watched him depart. "What a total dickhead. No wonder the HOA fees are so high."

Chapter 6

Ava's phone rang as she shifted into reverse and started backing out of the parking space. She answered. "Hi, Marilyn. I've just arrived and I'm on the way to get groceries." She slowed the car as she approached a yield sign. "I can't wait to see you." She had met Marilyn on the beach during one of her family's annual trips to the island. The petite outgoing blonde had been a foil to Ava's tall build and more reserved personality. They had become firm friends while hunting for shark's teeth in the sand despite the unwritten rule that "locals" didn't mix with tourists. Both girls had kept in touch and renewed their friendship every summer.

"Me too. I wanted to invite you for coffee tomorrow. The kids will be at day camp and I'll be free around two p.m."

"Sounds great. The Victoria City coffeehouse?" The café was in the small downtown area and next to the marina.

"Of course. Where else?" Marilyn paused. "I, uh, also kind of have a favor to ask."

Ava's pulse quickened. "You know I'm happy to help you in any way I can. What do you need? I'm always up for babysitting if you want a date night."

Marilyn exhaled noisily. "We might take you up on the offer to watch the kids. It would be great to have a night to ourselves. But that's not what I wanted to ask you about. I don't know if I mentioned this before, but Mark is on retainer with Rutledge Properties. It's a local commercial and residential real estate firm. They handle lots of rentals on the island and Mark does all the electrical repairs for them. Getting the Rutledge contract has been great for Mark's business. Mark went to high school with the owner, Jack Rutledge. Anyway, Jack is searching for an accountant for a short-term assignment. And, uh, Mark kind of mentioned that you would be coming to the island, and one thing led to another, and he sort of volunteered you to meet with Jack." Marilyn's voice trailed off.

"You know there isn't much I wouldn't do to help you and Mark." Ava's hand fluttered to her neckline. "But I'm under contract, so unless he wants to hire my firm, I don't see how I can help. But I would be delighted to sign him up. In fact, that's one of the things I'm here to do. Client development."

"I'm really sorry." Her voice dropped to a whisper. "I don't think Jack is exploring moving his accounting services to a new firm. I think he simply has a short-term project in mind. I know—I know that was presumptuous of him, but Mark was only trying to help his old friend. To be honest, he wants to impress his boss. Your visit seemed serendipitous."

Ava winced at the hesitation in Marilyn's speech.

An "off-the-books" accounting job would violate the terms of her employment contract with Penmans. Any work she got belonged to them. But how could she say "no" to Marilyn? And, what are the odds that Penmans would find out? She was being a lousy friend. Is that who she was? Who she had become? Is that who she wanted to be? It's not all about putting her employer first.

"What does Jack Rutledge want?"

"Jack didn't go into details with Mark." Marilyn's voice was small. "If you just meet with Jack, I'm sure it will all become clear."

Ava swallowed the lump in her throat. She hated hearing Marilyn plead. "I spoke without thinking this through. Of course I'll meet with him, although I can't commit as I don't know what he wants. But I'll do my very best to help him."

Marilyn gave a shaky laugh. "Ava, you're a rock star! Thank you! I'll get details from Mark and call you back." Marilyn hesitated.

Ava groaned. "Okay, what else haven't you told me? What are you getting me into? Spill it."

"Um, well, nothing bad. It's just that—well, Jack does have a reputation for being difficult. Sort of arrogant, I guess. But Mark thinks the world of him." She faltered. "Whatever people say about his personal life—" She stopped, before continuing, "He's always professional at work."

Ava sighed. "Well, he won't be the first difficult client I've had.

Chapter 7

"You don't need me, Mr. Rutledge." Sympathy flashed across Ava's face. She surveyed the man frowning at her. Jack Rutledge dominated the room. Even sitting, she could tell he was well over six feet. Short brown hair emphasized the angles of his lean face. Crinkles at the corners of his sapphire-blue eyes suggested he was in his mid- or late-thirties. She studiously ignored the nervous flutters in her stomach. This was business. It wouldn't do to let herself be distracted. And if she needed another reminder, Marilyn's warning popped into her head. She blinked twice and returned her focus to what Jack was saying.

"Please, call me Jack. And may I call you Ava?"

She cleared her throat. "Of course. Please do."

"I don't need you?" He waved one arm in a "tell me more" gesture. "What do you think I need?" Rocking his high-backed black leather chair slowly, he waited for her response.

A pained look crossed her face.

This is worse than telling a client they owed back taxes to the IRS and then trying to get them to pay the bill for the consultation. That never ended well.

She marshalled her arguments. "It's my professional opinion that you need someone with more of an audit focus."

When he failed to respond, she pushed a stray

strand of long brown hair out of her face and continued. "Mr. Rutledge—Jack—if you suspect that one of your employees is embezzling, then a forensic accountant will have the type of investigative and analytical experience necessary to perform a proper audit. And they would be able to put together the evidence for prosecution. They could testify as an expert witness. I have done audits, but my specialty is federal income tax preparation for small- to medium-sized enterprises, and I'm not equipped to do a forensic audit. Not to mention, I'm on holiday and my time is limited. Of course, Penmans would be delighted to help you with all your accounting needs. We have a department that specializes in audits." She squelched a feeling of guilt at the blatant pitch for business. She was sure Marilyn would forgive her.

Jack folded his hands on the desk but didn't say anything. The silence stretched uncomfortably long. Ava shifted in her chair. She crossed and then uncrossed her legs.

Finally, Jack leaned forward. "Ava, I understood from Mark that you were considering refocusing your career and that you were on extended leave from your accountancy firm."

And there it is. The bullet. A shot center mass. There are no secrets in a s*mall town.*

"Well, yes. I'm using two weeks of accrued holiday both to relax but also to work on client development, as well as to attend a two-day accounting seminar." She hoped she sounded nonchalant. "I'm considering my current position. There are a lot of corporate politics involved." She put the best possible spin on her situation.

Jack's lips twisted in a self-satisfied smile before flattening. "This would be an ideal opportunity for you to explore other areas of accounting without a commitment. Also, as you can appreciate, I can't call in our usual accounting firm as this island is small and the need for confidentiality in this matter is absolute. I can't have rumors in the local business community that the Rutledges have been taken for a ride. It would do untold damage to our firm's reputation and weaken our position in our contract negotiations. If we lost business, I would have to lay off long-term employees." He paused. "Contractors as well. I'm not interested in the prosecution of the embezzler. I just want to stop the bleeding. Mark assured me that you could be trusted and that you were both talented and discreet."

She blanched at the veiled threat to Mark's job. However, there was no upside to confirming embezzlement for a client. No one was ever happy to have a mistake confirmed. "I understand, Jack. I just don't think I'm the best person for the job."

Jack's jaw clenched and he locked gazes with her. "I would really appreciate if you would do this favor for me. A few hours a day for two weeks, and any account irregularities could be identified. I know Mark would not have recommended you if you couldn't do the job. I'm prepared to pay you generously for the intrusion into your vacation time."

Ava broke eye contact and stared out the large plate glass window behind Jack. An infinity pool abutted the sand dunes which formed a barrier to the Atlantic Ocean.

Nice view, but no answers out there.

Stalling, she gazed around the room. A large

nautical map hung on the wall and an antique brass sextant sat in a prominent position on his desk.

Stop delaying. There is no good decision here. Refuse to assist and irritate Mark's employer. Marilyn and Mark are financially dependent on the Rutledge Company for a lot of Mark's work. But no one considers the logical outcome of an audit. The client always blames the messenger. And by extension since they had recommended her, Mark and Marilyn would take some heat.

"Well, Ava?" Jack prompted.

She shifted in her chair. *No postponing the inevitable.* "You understand I'm not a forensic accountant?"

"Of course. But you are still qualified to do an audit."

Her shoulders slumped. "All right, then. I'll do my best to identify any irregularities in your accounts. If you accept these limitations, then I'll help you. When do you want me to start?"

"Thank you." Jack stood up abruptly. "How about tomorrow? I don't want any of the accounts to go off-site so it would be best if you worked out of the office in my house. My assistant Rachel is on vacation. You can use her desk." He gestured to the sleek modern pedestal desk that was positioned at ninety degrees to his. "Shall we say nine a.m. tomorrow?"

Ava stood up and smoothed the skirt of her sundress. "I'll see you then."

Chapter 8

She thought about tomorrow's schedule while she fished in her bag for the keys as she walked up the path to her front door. She could fit a few hours reviewing Jack Rutledge's accounts before she met Marilyn for coffee. And she could still make it to the Victoria City Marina cocktail party. Traditionally, the local marina always held a party to kick off the festivities for the Victoria Island Boat Show.

As she approached the entryway, she gagged as a foul smell overtook her. Covering her nose with her forearm, she hunted for the source of the odor. A shoe-box sized package was tucked behind the large planter that housed a Majesty palm. Flies buzzed around the brown cardboard box. She backed up and pulled out her phone. She opened her contacts list and called her mother.

"Hi, Mom."

"Hello, Ava, dear. How is everything?"

"Everything is fine, Mom. I'll call to chat later, but right now I just have a quick question. Are you expecting any deliveries here?"

"Well, no, of course not. We wouldn't be there to accept delivery."

"That's what I thought. Thanks, Mom. I'll give you a call later."

"I'll look forward to it, dear. Love you."

"Love you, too. Bye for now." She hung up and scrolled down to the security number.

Security picked up on the third ring. "Beaches Security. How can we help?"

"This is Ava Morrison, at Windward villas. I've had a suspicious delivery and wondered if you would send someone out?"

"What do you mean by suspicious?"

"It smells and it's attracting flies."

"Did you order any food and maybe forget to take it inside?"

"No, definitely not." Her response was quick and decisive.

"All right, ma'am. We'll send someone right over to investigate."

"Thanks." She went back down the path to wait. Her blouse stuck to her skin and she pulled it away before swatting at a gnat. The late afternoon heat was sweltering and the bugs, sensing a storm coming, circled at a low level. A few minutes later a white security SUV pulled into the lot and parked next to her car. Officer Thornley got out of the vehicle.

Just my luck. That officious little toad. She forced a polite smile on her face as he approached.

He lowered his dark aviator glasses a fraction and peered at her over the top rim. "What seems to be the problem, Ms. Morrison?"

"Could you examine this package? It smells. And no one in my family ordered anything."

"Are you sure about that? Sometimes people order food and then let it sit in the heat. The food spoils."

She clenched her teeth. "Dispatch already asked me that. I'm sure that no one ordered anything." Her voice sharpened. "Could you just take a look, please?" She winced at her shrill tone. He was only doing his job. He had asked a reasonable question. She tried for a more conciliatory tone. "I'd really appreciate it."

He held his hands up as if to mollify her. "No problem, ma'am. We're here to help."

"Great, thank you." She clenched her fists. "And could you please stop calling me 'ma'am.' "

"Yes, of course, ma'am."

She opened her mouth to object but then thought better of it. She was fighting a losing battle. No point making a further issue of it.

He followed her up the path and put his hand over his nose before bending down to view the package. He stood up and nudged it with his foot.

"Any breakables in there?"

"I told you. I didn't order it. So I have no idea."

He nudged the box out of the entryway and halfway down the path. He pulled a utility knife off his leather belt. Still holding one arm over his nose, he cut the seal of the package. He used the knife to flip back the lid. The open box revealed a pile of dog excrement. Officer Thornley sniggered. "Have you pissed off anyone lately?"

"No, of course not." Horrified, she shook her head back and forth. "I have no idea why someone would do this."

He held his focus. "Are you sure about that?"

"Of course, I am," she muttered in an irritated voice. "I prepare income tax returns for a living, for goodness' sake. How dull is that?"

He raised an eyebrow.

"Huh. I guess I kind of see your point. Well, no

client is upset with me that I'm aware of. And if they were, they wouldn't know to send this to my parents' address."

Nodding, he accepted her logic. "That makes sense." He pulled out his phone and snapped pictures of the box and its contents. Then he flipped over the box lid to get a picture of the address label and return label. "It's addressed to you."

"That doesn't make it my fault!"

He cocked his head. "Ex-boyfriend?"

"No. I mean, no one that would do this."

He gestured to the box. "Do you want to report this to the police?"

Ava shook her head. "I don't think so. I mean, what could they do?"

"Not much, I'm afraid. They could fingerprint the box, but as this is a nonviolent offense, this would be a low priority. You rent out your unit, right?"

She nodded.

"Maybe an unhappy renter? People do weird things, sometimes."

"Well—we have had some negative reviews. I suppose it is possible…"

"That's it, then." He flicked his knife shut and affixed it to his belt. "If you don't want to report it, I'll dispose of it. I've got a garbage bag in my vehicle."

"Thanks." She smiled tightly. "I'd appreciate that."

"Just part of the service, ma'am." He returned to his transport and retrieved a trash bag. Turning his head away from the smell, he opened the bag and pushed the box in with his foot. He quickly closed it up and carried the bag around the side of the building and threw it in the trash dumpster. He waved as he hurried back to his SUV and sped away.

Chapter 9

The early morning sun streamed through the window blinds and woke Ava. Yawning, she pushed the covers back and winced at the crick in her neck. She turned her head from side to side to work out the kinks. What should she wear on the first day? Opening the closet, she rummaged through the clothes she had brought. She pulled out a pale-pink sleeveless blouse with a deep V-neck. Hmm. Too revealing. Putting the blouse back, she flicked through the hangers. After a moment she chose a sleeveless white blouse with a Peter Pan collar and black pants. She added a cardigan to stay comfortable in the air-conditioned house and a pair of dressier sandals. Beep. She glanced at her phone and noted the time. Damn. She had better hurry. She rummaged in her purse searching for the keys. Darn it. Not now. Her gaze darted around the entryway. Aha. She snatched the keys from the table in the entry way and rushed out the door.

Her phone pinged and she opened her text messages with one hand and clicked the car's remote with the other. A text message written in all caps from an unknown number appeared.

—YOU DON'T BELONG HERE.—

What the heck? Some people were not only rude but also stupid. Who sends a nasty message to the wrong number?

She deleted the text message and dropped her phone into her purse.

Ava navigated the short drive from her family's island home to Jack's house on Ocean Avenue. The road ran parallel to the water and she caught glimpses of the blue expanse as she drove by the waterfront mansions. She arrived at Jack's modern three-story beach-front home and parked on the driveway.

Property development is clearly profitable.

For a moment she gazed up at the rooftop garden.

Probably great views from up there.

She shook off her musings, grabbed her purse and briefcase, and strode toward the house. The front door swung inward, and a large black Labrador propelled itself toward her. A woman with curly blonde hair in black culottes and a silk tank hurried out behind it. They both skidded to a halt.

The woman beamed at her while yanking on the dog's leash as he strained to reach Ava. "Hi, I'm Emma, Jack's sister."

"Hello, I'm Ava. It's a pleasure to meet you." She paused, not sure how much else to say, before continuing. "I have a meeting with Jack this morning." She held out her hand to shake hands. "And who is this?" The black dog's teeth were clenched around a blue rubber ball and he dribbled slobber. He wagged his tail violently.

Emma affectionately ruffled the fur on his neck. "This handsome guy is Zeus. He belongs to Jack, but I often pick him up to take him to doggy daycare when Jack has a lot of meetings." Zeus nudged Ava's hand and she leaned down to pet him.

Emma tilted her head. "Have you known Jack

long?"

"Actually, no, a friend of mine works for Jack and recommended me to him for a small project."

Jack appeared in the open doorway. "Hi, Ava." Jack came out onto the driveway. "I see you've met Emma and Zeus."

"Yes."

"Good. Well, I don't want to hold you up, Emma." Jack's smile slipped. "I know you want to get Zeus to daycare."

"Say no more, Jack. I get the hint." Emma opened the back of her white SUV and Zeus jumped in. "Zeus and I are leaving. I'll bring him back late this afternoon. They're having a pool party at doggy daycare and you know he loves those." Emma waved as she pulled out of the driveway.

"Come on in." He gestured for her to lead the way. "I hope I won't bother you while you work on the audit. I have some meetings offsite later this morning, so it should be reasonably quiet." He opened the door to the study.

"That sounds fine, Jack. Thank you." Ava examined the stylish desk located at the side of the large room. It was positioned facing outward into the room. Her back would be to a wall of bookshelves. The occupant would have a side view out the large window behind Jack's desk. A computer and printer sat on the modern glass top. She set her bag down on the desk and put her sweater on the back of the chair.

"Before we get started, let me show you around the house." Jack guided her with a hand low on her back into a large white kitchen. An oversized island of dramatic black-and-white zebra-patterned granite dominated the room. Bright gleaming stainless-steel appliances filled the kitchen. He pointed to a cabinet. "The coffee and tea are stored in there. Help yourself at any time. My housekeeper, Elsa, comes in from nine in the morning to one in the afternoon and she can also get you anything you need." He glanced at his watch. "She should be here shortly. She was picking up my dry cleaning."

"Thanks. I'm sure I can find my way around."

He led her out of the kitchen and down the hall. "The guest bathroom is down this hallway to the right." He showed her a stylish half-bathroom, with a mosaic tile pattern on the floor. "And, of course, you know the way to my office."

She smiled politely. "I'm sure I have everything I need, thanks." She moved her purse and briefcase to the floor under the desk. She looked up when a blast of cold air hit her. The desk was positioned directly under an air conditioning vent. She put on her cardigan and sat down.

"Well, good. Let me get you set up on the computer, with access to the accounts, and answer any questions you might have." He leaned his hip on the side of her desk and handed her a slip of paper. "This is the username and password I set up for you."

She powered on the computer. "Tell me about your accounts receivable and payable process."

"Emma, whom you met, and Matt, my brother, each head up a division of the company. Emma handles residential sales and Matt is in charge of property management. They each have a bookkeeper who reports to them."

"And who balances the books for the company

overall?"

"Rachel, my assistant, reconciles the account information she receives from both Emma and Matt. You'll meet Rachel when she gets back from her cruise. She is a friend of Emma's and has been my personal assistant for the past two years. Rachel also pays general bills related to the umbrella company." Jack leaned over her shoulder and logged in to the accounts on the computer on Rachel's desk. "I rely a lot on Rachel; she has proven to be a valuable addition to the company."

Ava gave a crisp nod. "I know how much of an asset a good administrative assistant can be. My assistant, Wendy, makes my life so much easier in so many ways. That gives me a general idea of the process, thanks. I'll review the computer accounts today and see if anything jumps out to me. It could simply be a math error."

Jack's features were set in grim lines. "It could be, although my gut tells me it's not. But I'll hold judgment until I have your findings and conclusion."

Elsa knocked on the door of the study before opening it and poking her head in. "Evelyn is here for you, Jack."

A slim woman in her thirties wearing a red clinging sheath dress teetered into the room on high-heeled color-matching sandals. The scent of an exotic perfume surrounded her. Her blonde hair was styled in an elegant French twist. "Jack, darling, how are you?" She threw her arms around him and kissed him on the cheek.

"Evelyn, it's nice to see you. You look lovely as always." Jack removed her arms from around his neck and gestured toward Ava. "Let me introduce you to Ava. She's doing some work for Rutledge's."

Evelyn turned toward Ava and gave her a perfunctory smile. "It's nice to meet you."

"Likewise." Shoulders hunched, Ava turned back to the keyboard. He was handsome and wealthy so of course he would have a beautiful girlfriend.

The social niceties satisfied, Evelyn turned back to Jack. "Jack, we'd better get going. I hate to be late when this is such a hot property." She put her hand on his arm. "You know how long I have been wanting to find just the right investment."

"Of course." Jack turned to Ava and handed her his business card. "Call me on my cell phone if you have any questions. I'll be back in a couple hours."

Chapter 10

Ava clicked on File Manager and opened the file with the accounts.

Scrolling down the financial entries, she scrutinized each line for any obvious signs of money being diverted away from any of the Rutledge accounts. She blinked. No unexplained withdrawals. No suspicious transfers. She opened a second file. One by one she compared bank account entries with the invoices in the second file. She rolled her shoulders. The business had a lot of transactions.

If it had been obvious, Jack would have found it. This won't be quick.

She began to compare vendor addresses on invoices with addresses found in internet searches but didn't find any made-up businesses. At twelve thirty she leaned back and rubbed her aching neck.

I definitely need to get to yoga classes. My muscles are as contorted as a pretzel. Time for a break.

She got up in search of Jack's housekeeper. Wandering into the kitchen, she found Elsa putting last minute touches to a Greek salad. A delicious smelling quiche sat cooling on the counter.

Elsa glanced up at her and smiled. "Jack should be back any minute. Would you like anything to drink?"

"Your coffee has been delicious but I think I hit my caffeine limit. But some water would be nice."

"Of course. Please, have a seat, and I'll get it for you."

"Thanks." Ava pulled out one of the high-backed bar stools and sat at the kitchen island. She had learned earlier that morning that Elsa liked to be the master of the kitchen.

"Have you worked for Jack long?"

Elsa sliced up a lime for Ava's water. "About five years, now. It's a very convenient part-time job which allows me time to work on my art."

"What kind of artist are you?"

"I work mostly with watercolors. Scenes of the island, local wildlife, etc. It sells well to tourists at the farmer's market downtown. The seascape in Jack's office is my work."

"Oh, I noticed that. It's lovely. I'll have to make a point of getting to the farmer's market to see more of your art."

"I'll watch out for you there." Elsa put a glass of sparkling water garnished with lime in front of Ava. She cocked her head. "That sounds like Jack's car now."

A minute later the door from the garage opened. The sound of footsteps echoed on the white marble floor.

"Hi, Elsa, Ava." He yanked at the knot in his tie. "It's a hot one out there."

"Hi, Jack. I was just on my way out for the day. I'll see you tomorrow," Ava said.

Jack glanced at his watch. "Could I have a quick word with you in the study before you go?"

"Of course." Ava's cell phone beeped and she glanced at her text messages.

—Go home, bitch. You don't belong here.—

She winced. Another damn text message from some anonymous coward. She noted that it was from a local number.

He waved a hand toward her phone. "Bad news?"

She shook her head "No, it's nothing." She put her cell phone back in her purse, her hand shaking slightly. She shouldn't let some creepy message get to her.

Jack closed the study door behind her.

"So, what news do you have for me?" He massaged his temples.

"Jack," Ava cleared her throat. "I think you need to have realistic expectations about this process. Auditing takes time. I'm in the process of checking verified receipts against the accounts. As you know, there are lots of receipts. You basically run three separate companies—property development, real estate sales, and rental management. That leaves a lot of scope for hiding embezzlement."

Jack spread his hands in a conciliatory gesture. "I apologize. I'm not a patient man. I do know a diligent audit will take time. Part of me was hoping that you would uncover the reason for the irregularities fairly quickly. I don't like to think that someone on my staff is stealing money from the company. Of course, if it was obvious, I would wonder why I hadn't found the problem myself. I guess you can't win with me, can you?" A pained expression marred his face.

Ava's face softened. 'It's not a nice feeling, is it? To think that someone you trust is taking advantage of you." *It's not about the money.* She had seen enough of the Rutledge accounts to know the missing funds were not significant to the financial health of the business, but it clearly bothered Jack. "It can't be easy to have an employee violate your trust." It was probably worse since it was a family-owned company with a small number of employees.

"No, it's not easy." He grimaced. "I built this company from nothing. My family had owned some land here for many years. Everyone wrote the land off as worthless."

She lifted one eyebrow. "But you thought differently?

"Maybe I'm just too stubborn to listen to people." It was his turn to shrug. "I took a calculated risk and it paid off. When I returned after college, I got my realtor's license, and then my broker's license, and developed some of the land we owned into a shopping center. The Rutledge Company grew from there. We've now expanded into rental property management in addition to commercial property development. Victoria Island has a thriving economy and is growing quickly which is good for business. It's a resilient business model. In the boom times, the property development and real estate sales thrive. In a recession, the rental management company does well. It's been good for our family."

"It must be nice to work with family."

"It is. I can always count on Matt and Emma to be frank and honest with me. The downside is that I'm responsible for their livelihoods. And sometimes it's hard not to treat them as my younger siblings instead of the accomplished real estate professionals that they are."

"You've known Mark since high school?"

"We were in the same class. We played baseball

together. Some good times." A knock sounded and a cold draft from the air conditioning hit them as Elsa opened the door.

"Jack, you have a telephone call. It's Evelyn. She says she needs to talk to you about her latest charity fundraiser."

A flash of exasperation crossed Jack's face. "She could have mentioned that earlier. Tell her I'll be right with her."

"And that's my cue to go." Ava picked up her handbag. "I'll see you tomorrow."

Chapter 11

Guests in yacht-casual wear carrying handcrafted cocktails milled around the outdoor deck of the Victoria City Marina. The indoor-outdoor venue was decorated with festive lights which reflected off the water. The wet slips were full of elegant speedboats, catamarans, and fishing vessels. Buildings with oversized garage doors housed the dry docks and lined the periphery of the property.

Ava discreetly adjusted the deep V-neck of her pale yellow sleeveless maxi dress. A silver starfish pendant and matching earrings finished her outfit. A waiter walked by and Ava picked a glass of what appeared to be a mojito off his tray. She shifted her weight as her high-heeled sandals pinched her toes. Ignoring the pain in her feet, she scanned the room for any familiar faces. Many people her father worked with used this marina for their hobby boats. She might not be able to sign one of them, but they could be useful for introducing her around.

A stately older man with thinning gray hair caught her eye and waved. A slender woman of indeterminate age stood next to him. Her blonde hair was coiled in an elegant chignon. Brendan and Charlene Myrtle. Perfect. Just the people to help her mingle. Long-time clients of her father's law firm and established family friends.

She waved back and weaved her way across the

crowded room toward the distinguished-looking couple.

"Charlene, Brendan! It's so nice to see you."

Charlene enveloped her in a hug. "Ava, it's been too long. How are you?'

"I'm doing well. How are you both?"

Charlene put her hand on her husband's arm. "We're good. But I had a terrible time pulling Brendan away from work to come down here. He's always stuck in one of his projects. There's no point having a boat if you never use it, now is there?"

Brendan smiled indulgently. "Now, honey, you act as if I never take time off."

"Well, you work too hard, darling." Charlene turned to Ava. "Did your parents come down as well?"

"No, unfortunately not. They'll be here for the July 4th festivities though."

"That's wonderful. We'll be here as well. I'm going to contact Lilian and make plans. Maybe we can take a sunset cruise on Brendan's new toy." She pointed to a fifty-foot yacht.

"Wow, Brendan. That is some boat. Whatever project you've been working on clearly has been successful."

A playful twinkle appeared in his eye. "I'm enjoying it. Now, if only your father could find a way to make it tax deductible."

Charlene shook her head in mock despair. "Brendan is still trying to find a way to make *me* tax deductible. Anyway, do you have plans for your visit, Ava?"

"I'm here for a mix of vacation and client development. I'm hoping to find some clients at one of the boat festival parties."

"You've come to the right place." Charlene linked her arm with Ava's. "Let me introduce you around. Maybe I can help you find a client." She patted Ava's hand. "Or a husband. Lillian would owe me. Now tell me, what are you going to wear to woo these potential new clients?"

"I brought a black sleeveless sheath dress with me."

Charlene winced. "Not that old dress you pull out for corporate functions? The one that says 'I'm a number cruncher and I'll just stand in the corner?' "

"Well, uh, yes. And I am a number cruncher. It's appropriate for all parties."

"No, honey. You've got an amazing opportunity. You've got to stand out from the crowd. You can't dress like an accountant. Not in these circles. If you have any chance of signing a client, you need to exude 'old money' or at least 'lots of money.' You need to go shopping. There's a darling boutique downtown. I've found lots of beautiful clothes there. You really must pay it a visit. I'll let Eleanor, the manager, know that you'll be in. She'll fix you up with something appropriate for these high-flyer events."

"Don't pressure her, Charlene," Brendan admonished. "While you ladies 'work the room,' I'm going to have a word with Charles Ormsby. He's planning an inland cruise up the intracoastal. I want to hear all about it."

"Thanks, Charlene. But I'll give you fair warning. The only market I'm in at the moment is the business one. Lead the way."

Chapter 12

Ava sat at the kitchen island, her hands encircling a coffee mug. Still dressed in her workout tights and sports bra, she glanced at her watch. Damn it. Eight o'clock already. She had lingered too long enjoying her caffeine fix and doom scrolling. Now she would need to hurry and change or she would be late for the continuing education seminar.

Someone rapped on the front door. Irritated, she put down her coffee mug and hurried to answer the door. She couldn't afford any delays. Despite the island only being thirteen miles long, it was a thirty-minute drive downtown to the hotel where lectures were being held when traffic was good. And that didn't factor in tourists who drove golf carts on the roads. The vehicles were limited to twenty-five miles per hour yet they drove them on roads with higher speed limits. Car drivers got frustrated with the slow-moving carts and did stupid things. And she didn't know what was going on this weekend that might impact the traffic. The island's businesses usually sponsored some event to attract day-trippers.

She opened the door and her eyes widened. "Toby, what on earth are you doing here?" She pulled a face. "And how did you know where I was?"

"You didn't return any of my calls or texts, so I had to come see you in person." Ava winced, recalling the messages she had ignored. Toby shouldered his way through the front door. "I convinced the new clerk in Human Resources to give me your address. I was sure you wouldn't mind. Isn't it great? I signed up for the continuing education seminar and will be here through the weekend. We could talk tonight over dinner. We have a lot to catch up on."

"Uh, I don't know, Toby." Ava opened and closed her mouth like a hungry fish hunting for food. She struggled to find the right words. "I'm not really sure we have anything to talk about." She made a mental note to have a frank discussion with HR about giving out private information.

"Don't be like that, Ava." Toby's expression soured. "We have lots to talk about."

Had he always been that way or was she just noticing? "Hey, I'm sure that we'll have time to talk later. We can catch up on a coffee break during the class." She held up her hands in a placating gesture. "I have to shower and change. I'll see you at the seminar downtown at nine."

"Great, I'll see you soon." A self-satisfied smile in place, Toby gave her a kiss on the cheek and turned around to go back to his rental car. Ava shut the door and leaned against it. How was she going to avoid meeting up with him? Probably something she couldn't dodge. Better to just get it over with. She locked the door and went down the hallway to get dressed.

Ava's cell phone rang. Wendy's number appeared on the screen. Her administrative assistant. She hit the answer button. "Hi, Wendy."

"Hi, Ava, sorry to bother you while you're on vacation, and especially on a Saturday, but I wanted to give you a heads up about something. I tried to get in touch with you yesterday but your cell phone just rang and rang."

"I had some missed calls, but they came up as an unknown number. I don't know why your calls didn't go to voicemail. Anyway, no worries, what's up?"

"The company found some money left over from last quarter for training. Toby and a few others, including Sheila, are headed to Victoria Island to attend the advanced accounting seminar this weekend. I thought you would want to know."

"Thanks Wendy. It's fine. But I appreciate the heads up. It's a shame I missed your calls yesterday—I've just seen Toby. He turned up on my doorstep this morning."

"Oh, sorry about that. I was hoping to soften the blow."

"As I said, no worries. Enjoy your weekend!"

Ava picked up her leather open top satchel that served as her purse and a piece of paper fluttered out to the floor. Frowning, she leaned down to pick it up. It was folded so much it could have been origami. Curiously, she smoothed it out. *GO HOME. NO MORE WARNINGS.* Her fingers burned and she dropped the note. Where had that come from? She shuddered. The text messages were creepy but could have been a wrong number. But this...this was different.

Whoever wrote it had been close enough to drop the note in her bag.

Her legs shook and she sank down into the chair. This and the dog poo were personal. Someone was threatening her. She thought back through her day. No one had been near her bag. She used the same carryall at work. It was conceivable it was put in her bag in Atlanta and she just hadn't discovered it. But why? What did they want from her? To leave the island? Or to leave Penmans?

She wiped her clammy hands on her pants. *Should she call the police? What could she say?* She didn't know where or when the note was put into her bag. *And it's just a note.* Trembling, she dumped her bag out on the floor and sorted through everything. Nothing missing. She sat back in relief.

This time she blocked the number on her phone instead of merely deleting the text message and made a mental note to ask Security to patrol around their block more frequently.

Chapter 13

Ava arrived at the seminar twenty minutes after the class had started. It was the Saturday that the monthly farmer's market was held and all the available parking near the hotel had been taken. She had been forced to prowl up and down the side streets. Finally, she had lurked near a grassy area that had been turned into a temporary lot and waited for someone to leave. Zooming into the space as soon as the vehicle departed, she parked and locked her car. She rushed down the street to the hotel.

She hurried to the registration desk outside the main conference room. A perky blonde twenty-something whose badge announced her name as "Summer" in calligraphy greeted her with a lively "Welcome." She shifted her weight from foot to foot to ease the pressure on her soles while she waited for Summer to review the multi-sheet attendance list. She knew she would regret wearing high heels. Who was she trying to impress? And that race-walk from her car had been a killer. Finally, Summer ticked the box next to her name, skimmed over the seminar badges on the table, and handed hers to her along with her educational materials. With a quick thank you, she clipped the ID badge to the collar of her blouse and slipped into the auditorium.

A whoosh of cold air assaulted her as the air

conditioning strained to keep the room below freezing. Tables covered with white cloths were set up in rows and filled the cavernous space. Each participant had a large three ring binder with conference materials set in front of them. The instructor, who had a wireless microphone so that she could move around the room, clicked to the next slide in the presentation.

Ava surveyed the full room and headed to the back row to claim one of the few remaining empty seats. As she was sitting down, she caught a movement in the corner of her vision. Toby had leaned over and was whispering something to Sheila, who chuckled in response. Ava's eyes narrowed as she watched them. They seemed too cozy. Was Toby playing them both? To see whether she or Sheila would be better for his career? She hoped everyone in the office didn't see it. Whatever. Nothing she could do about it. She huffed out a loud breath and the man in the pinstripe suit sitting next to her shot her an annoyed glance. *Crap. I picked the seat next to an uptight partner. Who wears a suit for a weekend seminar?* She quickly looked away, squared her shoulders, and focused straight ahead. She had missed the introductory patter and the first lecturer was getting into the substance of the lecture.

The instructor droned on about upcoming changes in the tax laws. Taking copious notes, she mulled over the challenges these amendments would present for many of her clients. The complicated topic kept her mind off both Jack and Toby and the morning sessions passed quickly. When the class stopped for a break, she stepped out of the room to get a cup of coffee.

A table had been set up just outside the conference room. It held oversized flasks of regular and decaffeinated rapidly cooling coffee. A condiments tray held powdered creamer, sugar, and stir sticks. At the other end of the refreshment station, flasks held hot water and baskets with a selection of tea bags. Several plates holding an assortment of cookies had already been ravaged by the hungry horde. Ava poured coffee into a paper cup.

"Ava, nice to see you. I didn't realize you would be here." Sheila wore an ivory pantsuit with a matching shell. With her black hair cut into a bob, she appeared both sophisticated and successful. Partner material. Toby wore a sport coat over a polo and chinos.

Ava finished stirring powdered creamer into her coffee. She mulled over the wisdom, or lack thereof, of wearing her slim black pants and cardigan and the casual image she projected in contrast to Sheila, before turning to face them.

She forced a smile. "Hi, Sheila. I'm vacationing and decided to take advantage of this seminar. How are you enjoying the hotel?"

Sheila pushed back the sleeve of her silk jacket and checked the time on her gold watch before answering. "Unfortunately, we booked late, and there were no rooms left, so Toby and I are at the Marina Bed and Breakfast down the street."

Her cheeks were starting to hurt from the pressure of keeping her smile in place.

Say something pleasant even if it kills you.

"That sounds like a nice place to stay for the weekend."

"It is." Sheila leaned in closer to Ava. Her jet-black hair contrasted against her pale skin and red lipstick, reminding Ava of a character from a scary children's movie.

"Ava, I don't want there to be any hard feelings between us. I know you were disappointed at not being selected for my position. The partners just thought I was better qualified."

Ava gritted her teeth and hoped the noise wasn't audible. "Congratulations again on the promotion, Sheila. It's not a problem for us to work together. We're both professionals."

Sheila rested her hand on Ava's arm. "Well, that is very gracious of you, Ava. I'm sure you must be a pro at handling disappointment. After all, we can't all be management material."

Ava could almost hear the blood rushing to her head.

Let it go. Just let it go.

Sheila canvassed the room as if the conversation bored her. "Well, if you'll excuse me a minute, I see some people I need to say hello to before the break is over."

Toby kept his gaze somewhere between her and Sheila and did not make any eye contact.

She walked away, periodically giving a royal wave or gracious nod of her head to various attendees as she headed across the room.

Toby watched Sheila depart and then turned back to Ava, redness creeping up his neck. "It's not what you think."

"I'm not sure what is going on"—she held up a hand—"but I'm also positive that it's not any of my business."

"Now, Ava, don't be like that. I know things got a little complicated last week, but I think we have a lot to talk about."

"I disagree." She swirled her coffee in the cup. "I think you lost any interest in me when I didn't get the promotion."

"It wasn't like that at all," Toby protested. "Have dinner with me so I can explain."

What had she seen in him? *What a whiner. Sheila is welcome to him.*

"Come on Ava, it's just dinner."

Exasperated, she blew out a breath. No doubt he would go on and on until she agreed. And she didn't have any plans anyway. Maybe she could at least stick him with the bill. He deserved it. She cheered briefly at that thought before realizing he would be charging it to their employer. "Very well, Toby. We can have dinner after the seminar, but it will have to be quick. I've got errands to run."

"Great! I can't wait."

"Me, too," she said, a little too flatly. "People are heading back in. We should go back to our seats for the next session."

At five p.m., Ava walked out of the seminar with Toby. Sheila headed back toward the B and B, her cell phone glued to her ear and a somber "I'm talking to an important person" expression on her face. The downtown was buzzing with tourists and locals, both in search of happy hour specials and dinner. Taking her sweater off as the early evening heat hit them as they exited the hotel, Ava turned to Toby. "There's a bar and grill just a few blocks down the road. The food and service are better there than at many of the restaurants downtown. Most rely too much on tourists who don't stray off the main street."

"That sounds fine." He glanced at her. "I'm glad you made time to have dinner with me."

"Sure. Of course. Here it is." Ava gestured to a restaurant on the corner. Despite her assurances, *The Pirate's Lair* was crowded with both tourists and casually dressed locals. Patrons carried elaborate cocktails and mingled in the dimly lit bar. Televisions with closed captioning enabled hung on the walls and streamed various sporting events. The hostess wore a black T-shirt with a skull and crossbones and cutoff jean shorts. She led them to a table for two outside on the patio.

She dug a small notebook out of the back pocket of her shorts. "What can I get you, folks?"

Ava skimmed the wine list. "I'll have a glass of the house white wine."

The hostess turned to Toby. "And you, sir?"

Toby perused the drinks menu. "What temperature is your wine chilled at?"

One corner of her mouth pulled back before she assumed the blank look of a professional server. "Cool enough to be chilled but not frosted."

Toby snorted. "I'll have the local IPA."

Scribbling notes in her pad, she then stuffed it in her pocket. "Your server will have your drinks shortly."

When the waiter brought their drinks, Ava ordered a wedge salad with blue cheese dressing and Toby requested the "buccaneer burger" with seasoned steak fries.

"So." Ava put the menu aside. "What did you want to talk about?"

Toby smoothed his hair back. A fleeting expression that could have been nervousness flashed across his face "I'm really sorry you didn't get the promotion. The rumor around the office is that Sheila won out because she is better at client recruitment." He fixed her with a stare. "And they also are saying that Maggie gave you an ultimatum. Sign a big client or go."

Ava's eyes blazed. A surge of combined humiliation and rage welled up inside her. "If you really had been sorry, you wouldn't have cancelled our date. And as for rumors, I never pay attention to them. People love to talk but they seldom care whether what they are repeating is true or not." Fury consumed her. *Calm down. He's not worth it. You're overreacting.*

"Well, I—"

Ava held her hand up to stop him. "I'm sorry about that. I didn't mean to be snarky. It's just—well, I could have used a distraction and some cheering up. But that's in the past."

He rubbed the back of his neck. "I know. I can't say how sorry I am and that I regret how I handled it."

Ava scoffed. "The scuttlebutt around the office is that you went out with the group celebrating Sheila's promotion."

"Uh…" He reached for his beer and took a swallow. The door to the restaurant opened bringing with it a blast of artic air and they both turned toward the distraction. Jack and a younger man walked outside. They wore the ubiquitous island uniform of shorts and short sleeve polo shirts. Both had the same angular lines in their faces and lean bodies, suggesting a familial relationship. The younger man stopped to talk to a group at a nearby table. Jack glanced around the patio, saw her, and headed for their table.

His eyes lit up with an unknown emotion. "Hello,

Ava, I see you needed a drink after your seminar."

Ava's lips parted in a wide grin. "You have no idea."

Toby cleared his throat.

Ava started. "Oh, sorry. Toby, this is Jack Rutledge, a friend of mine. Jack, Toby is a colleague from Atlanta. He and a few other coworkers came down for the conference." Toby stood up to shake Jack's hand and then sat down again.

"Welcome to Victoria Island, Toby. Are you in town for long?" Jack's hands settled on the back of Ava's chair.

Toby leaned back and arched his neck to meet Jack's gaze. "I'm just here for the weekend, although I might extend my stay longer." Toby put his hand over Ava's. Ava slid her hand out from under Toby's, picked up her wine glass, and sipped.

The younger man approached their table with an easy smile. "This is my brother, Matt." Jack gestured toward the table. "Matt, this is Ava, a friend of mine, and her colleague Toby."

"It's a pleasure to meet you both," Matt's eyes sparked with interest as his gaze flicked between Jack and Ava.

Toby drummed his fingers on the table. "Rutledge. That name sounds familiar. Although I'm sure Ava has never mentioned you. Does Ava handle your accounts?"

"Uh, no. We're in property development and sales. You've probably seen our signs around the island. It's good to know our advertising is creating name recognition."

"Yes, that could be it. How long have you known

Ava?"

"Long enough." A vein throbbed in Jack's neck. "Well, we won't keep you. I'll see you soon, Ava."

Ava's chin dipped. "Yes, I'll see you around."

Ava watched as Jack and Matt left the restaurant's patio, then she turned back to Toby. Her eyes narrowed. "I have to ask you something and I want the truth."

Toby raised his hands. "Of course. I've never lied to you, Ava."

"Have you been sending me crazy text messages telling me to go home?"

"No, of course not!" He held his hands up as if warding her off. "I have no idea what you're talking about. "

Ava studied him before giving a curt nod. "Okay, then. I just had to ask."

"Tell me what's going on." He scooted his chair closer to the table and leaned forward.

She turned her wine glass around slowly and gazed at the table. "It's nothing. I've had these strange text messages." Suddenly parched, she picked up her water glass and drank. The liquid trickled down her throat. "I'm sure it's just a case of a mistaken phone number."

"Well, I'm sure it's nothing to worry about." Toby waved his hand dismissively. "Probably someone just drunk texting an ex."

She bristled and he held his hand up. "Hey, don't get me wrong. I'm not condoning it. No one should send angry text messages." He snorted. "I mean, it's just stupid, isn't it? There's bound to be a digital trail." Toby sampled his beer. "Anyway, you always did worry too much. Now, I'd love to see you while I'm here. It would be great to spend some time together—

just the two of us—away from all the stress of Atlanta. I could extend my stay and we could go to the beach on Monday. I've been watching the forecast. The weather will be good."

Ava fiddled with her napkin. "I don't know, Toby. I have a lot to take care of at my parents' condo." Ava signaled to the waiter for their check. "I'm glad that we had this dinner together." Picking up her wine glass, she swallowed the rest of the pinot grigio and set the glass down decisively. "I'll be back in Atlanta very soon. We can get together then."

"It's not the same." Toby's jaw tightened. "We need this time away together."

"Honestly, Toby, I have some thinking to do."

"Don't give up on us, Ava." Toby leaned across the table and picked up her hand, rubbing her palm with his thumb. "We're good together. We can have a successful future together."

"But we haven't—"

He shook his head. "Don't say another word. I'm extending my stay. We can find time together."

"Toby, I really can't make any promises."

"That's okay. I'm sure we can both find time. It's all about priorities, Ava. That was our problem in Atlanta. We didn't put each other first."

"You didn't answer my question, Toby."

Toby took another swig of his beer. "Sorry. I lost track there. What was your question?"

"Why did you cancel our date and go out with the crowd to celebrate Sheila's promotion?"

He leaned forward. "Ava, I hated to cancel our plans. I really did. But you must see that it was vital to be supportive of Sheila since she got the promotion.

You should have gone. Nobody likes a sore loser."

She leaned back in her chair. "Just because I didn't go out and celebrate when someone else got a promotion over me does not make me a sore loser," Ava retorted, her voice sharp.

"Corporate politics, Ava." He threw his hands up in a "what can you do" gesture. "We may not always like some of the things we have to do, but we need to show that we're team players. If you isolate yourself, you won't make the connections you need to succeed. That's how you get ahead. Hell, that's how you get ahead in life. We don't have to like it. But we do have to live with it."

"Whatever, Toby." Her cheeks burned. She hated that he may be right. "You made your choice that night. And I'm fine with that. I think we're better off as just friends."

"Now, Ava, there is no need for such a hasty decision. What we have together is great. We have so much in common. And when you get over this little hiccup you're having with Maggie, your career will get back on track."

"What we had together may have been good for a while, but I really think the time has passed."

"You're clearly still upset about everything." He reached into his back pocket to pull out his wallet. He put his company credit card on the table. "Why don't you sleep on it, and we can have lunch tomorrow?"

Ava surveilled the crowded restaurant while she pondered her response. "I don't know, Toby. I don't think I'm going to change my mind." She reached over the table and squeezed his hand. "For the first time in a while, things seem very clear to me."

Scribbling his name on the credit card receipt, he looked up at her. "We'll talk tomorrow."

"I won't change my mind. But call me tomorrow and I'll see if I'm free for lunch." *Huh. Maybe I'll be free for lunch if hell freezes over, you're the last man standing on earth, and if it's at a separate restaurant.*

Toby studied the line at the hostess station. A family with three children waited. The father looked around the patio in the search for a free table and a small child fidgeted but clung to her mother's hand. Two teenagers scrolled through their phones, oblivious to their surroundings. "Tables are at a premium right now. Come on. I'll walk you to your car."

Ava pushed back her chair and stood up. "Thanks, Toby, but I'm just a few blocks down the street, and your bed and breakfast is in the opposite direction. It's perfectly safe here."

"Well, if you insist. I'll say goodnight." Toby leaned forward to give her a kiss, but Ava tilted her head at the last minute and Toby's kiss landed on her cheek instead.

"See you tomorrow."

"Good night, Toby."

Chapter 14

"Hey, Jack, there was no need to rush off." Matt lengthened his stride, weaving through the crowded sidewalk, dodging tourists who loitered outside restaurants reading the menu boards, and caught up to Jack. Sunburned teenagers congregated in a group outside the ice cream shop. "We could have had a drink with them, you know."

Jack chose to forget the burst of jealousy he felt when he had seen Ava with another man. What was it about her that made him keep thinking about her? "I didn't want to intrude." Jack skirted around a dog lifting its leg to pee on a "keep off the grass" sign while its owner held the leash and pretended not to notice.

"So how long have you known Ava?" Matt asked. "She seems nice. Pretty, too," he added, with a sly glance in Jack's direction. "And not at all like Janice."

"Why on earth are you bringing Janice up?" Annoyance flashed across Jack's face. He fished in his pocket for his keys.

"Because, big brother, whether you realize it or not, you assume every woman is like Janice. You're thirty-eight and you never let a woman get too close. As soon as a fling seems to be evolving into a relationship, you dump the woman," Matt retorted.

Memories assailed him. A vision of his former fiancée wrapped in his arms, whispering her love for him, morphed into her naked and moaning underneath a fraternity brother. They had dated for the last two years of college and had been planning a future together. His mind raced. Their relationship was destroyed in a moment. Or possibly the life they planned never existed. Maybe he had just built Janice up to be someone she wasn't. Jack pushed those thoughts to the back of his mind. "No. I don't," he replied curtly. "And to answer your question, not long. She's helping me with an accounting issue."

"If that is what you want to call it, big brother!" Matt smirked. "It's good to see you back on the market. It's been a while. Emma and I have been worried that you are turning into a recluse. We figure we'll show up at your house one day, and you'll have long white hair and a shaggy beard, dressed in ragged clothes, and we'll find you counting stacks of money in your office."

"I'm not becoming a hermit," he said as he picked a leaf off the windscreen. "Or a miser. I just don't date as much as you do." He snorted. "In fact, at my advanced age, I couldn't possibly date as many women as you do, Matt. Actually, I couldn't keep up with you at any age. How do you keep them straight?"

Matt made a face. "Very funny. But relax. She wasn't into that guy. She was freezing him out."

"If I were interested, that would be good to know." He wondered who he was trying to convince. Matt or himself? His gaze swept the area. "But I'm not, so it's irrelevant. According to Mark, Ava's a 'settle-down' kind of woman. And I have to agree with his assessment. I can spot them a mile away. She gives off nesting vibes. That's not on my agenda. It would be a mistake to get involved with her. And anyway, she is a business partner at the moment."

"Sure, sure." Matt held his hands up. "Whatever you say, Jack. Let's get going. You can drop me off and then I'll call Emma to update her."

Jack cuffed Matt on the side of the head. "Get in the car."

Chapter 15

Brendan pulled the luxury sedan forward in the long line of cars waiting to get to the temporary valet station at the front of the waterfront mansion. The tailback of guests' cars blocked the U-shaped drive and continued out into the road, halting traffic. Private security officers used hand signals and directed traffic.

"Keep your eye on the car in front, Brendan," Charlene warned.

"It's hard to do. Look at that car!" He jabbed a finger at a vehicle double-parked several cars ahead. "I think it's that limited edition Italian sports car. You know, it debuted at the race in Monte Carlo last year. It's taken the racing world by storm."

"Well, try harder to watch traffic. If you crunch the fender of that car in front of us, you're going to have to sell your boat to pay the bill. And for goodness sakes, don't point. People will think we're tourists."

Ava smothered a giggle and peered out the side window to get a better view of the sports car.

Charlene shook her head. "Ava, I don't care how old or successful a man is. They never outgrow their fascination with cars."

"I can't thank you both enough for getting me an invitation."

"Oh, it was our pleasure, dear. And it was no trouble, really. I'm on the steering committee for the VI

Arts Festival with Jacklyn, Bernard's wife," Charlene said.

"Nevertheless, I'm so appreciative."

Brendan inched the car forward. "And just take a gander at that house. It's huge. The oceanfront lot alone must have cost in the multi-millions."

"Honestly, Brendan, your bourgeois roots are showing."

He grinned. "You love me and my middle-class upbringing."

Ava leaned back in the rear seat. Brendan and Charlene had been high school sweethearts. Brendan did not come from a monied background, and Charlene had married him over her wealthy parents' objections. A few years into their marriage, Brendan had patented a fix for a troubled automated manufacturing process and the money had rolled in. Despite their immense wealth, they had kept their down-to-earth attitudes.

Ava thought about the two cocktail dresses that Charlene had helped her pick out. One was a red one-shoulder slim-fit sheath with a long slit exposing one leg. The other was a cornflower-blue halter-neck midi dress, which she wore tonight. She refused to think about the dent in her bank account. Elegance did not come cheaply. She hoped Charlene was right that she needed these clothes to fit in.

The four-story beach-front residence sat behind wrought-iron gates and covered three lots. It had a vaguely Italian-style architecture with red clay roof tiles. Ornate columns embellished the exterior. An imperial staircase with its divided stairway led to massive double doors.

"I can't wait to see the inside," Charlene

commented. "I understand that Jacklyn brought in an interior designer from Milan. I bet it's fabulous in an over-the-top neo-classical Italian sort of way."

Brendan chuckled. "Now who is being a tourist?"

"Well, okay, maybe just a little." She cast him a loving glance. "But I'll be discreet about it." She turned to Ava. "What is the best way to help you, Ava?"

"If you could introduce me around, I'd appreciate it. I'll try not to embarrass you with a hard sell."

"Just do what you have to do, Ava. We're in your corner." The car crawled forward. "Finally, we're at the front."

Brendan handed his keys to the valet and they all got out of the car. Due to the number of guests, cars were being parked at an off-site location. Ava followed Brendan and Charlene up the stairs.

"On behalf of Mr. and Mrs. Wallington, welcome." An assistant stood at the entryway with a clipboard and marked off their names on the guest list.

They filed into the entry way. A string quartet played Vivaldi in the corner of the large living room. The mayor and her husband sat on one of a pair of white suede leather sofas separated by an oversized black-and-white marble-top coffee table with lacquer base. Bernard and Jacklyn sat opposite but stood up as they entered the room.

"Charlene! How delightful. And you must be Brendan." Jacklyn and Charlene exchanged air kisses. "I'm so glad you were able to come."

"Bernard, Jacklyn, this is our dear friend, Ava Morrison."

Bernard waved his hands expansively. "Welcome to our little soiree. Please, help yourself to a drink and mingle. We'll catch up later."

"Thank you. We'll look forward to it." Brendan steered both ladies out to the grand patio. A wooden boardwalk was suspended over the protected sand dunes and led to the beach. The large space was tiled and had been transformed into a dance floor. Another band played. Couples danced with varying levels of skill. They traversed the edge of the terrace.

Charlene leaned toward Brendan and whispered, "I see Julia and Marlon over there. We've got to say hello." She turned to Ava. "Will you excuse us for just a minute?"

Ava shooed them off. "I'll be fine."

"I thought I'd never get you alone." A man with his blond hair gelled back and wearing a pink button-down oxford shirt with the sleeves rolled up and khaki paints held a glass of champagne out to her. "I'm Rob Welton."

"Thank you. I'm Ava Morrison." She accepted the proffered glass as a prop. She never drank out of a glass that she hadn't seen poured no matter how swank the gathering.

"I haven't seen you at one of Bernard and Jacklyn's parties before. How do you know our hosts?"

Ava gestured across the room. "Charlene Myrtle, a family friend, sits on a board with Jacklyn. I don't live on the island. I'm visiting from Atlanta for a few weeks. How do you know them?"

"I work with Bernard in finance. I've been to several of his parties here. Let me give you a tour of the house. It has to be seen to be believed." He took her arm and led her back into the house. "Bernard and Jacklyn were inspired by their Italian trips. The interior is modeled after a palazzo in Venice."

"I didn't know that. They've certainly achieved a beautiful home." Ava smiled encouragingly.

He pointed at the intricate chandelier. "The light fixtures were handmade in Murano. Come, let me show you the curated art collection. It's Jacklyn's pride and joy."

"Is that a little like showing me your etchings?"

Rob burst out laughing. "Bernard would fire me if I made a move on one of his guests. These little get-togethers may have a social veneer but they are all about business."

"Good to know."

Rob opened the door to the library and ushered her in. He pointed to several oil paintings hanging on the wall under gallery lights. "These were bought on the recommendation of a museum curator friend. They're great investments. All up and coming artists."

She slanted him a glance. "Bernard is not a fan of bitcoin investing?"

"Nah. He is kind of old school. Can't go wrong with real estate and artwork."

She studied the largest one. The abstract painting was a fusion of colors. "On the one hand, it appears as if the artist just splashed paint on the canvas. But it's soothing somehow. And I'm pretty sure I couldn't replicate the effect."

"It is a conundrum, isn't it? How something so random manages to be thought- provoking?"

They turned as another couple came into the library. Jack Rutledge and Evelyn stopped just inside the doorway.

"I hope we're not interrupting," Jack murmured.

A flash of an emotion that could have been pain crossed Rob's face but was quickly masked. "Not at all, Jack, Evelyn. Good to see you both. This is Ava."

"Nice to see you, Rob. Ava, lovely to see you again," Jack said quietly.

"Rob, it's been too long." Evelyn leaned in and kissed his cheek. "You owe me a dance after leaving the Christmas party so early."

"I do. And I always make good on my promises." He turned to Ava. "Would you excuse me?"

"Of course. Thanks for the tour."

Rob and Evelyn headed back outside to the makeshift dance floor.

"I didn't realize you knew the Wallingtons." Heat flashed in Jack's eyes. "You look lovely this evening."

A flush crept up her neck. "Thank you." She felt like a 1950s movie star in the blue midi dress. Charlene's recommendation had been perfect. She fit right in with the other guests. She searched for something to say to fill the conversational void.

"How do you know Bernard, Jack?"

Jack's eyes twinkled. "I sold him this property."

"Oh! Nice commission if you can get it."

"Yes, it was. Particularly since this house is on three lots. But Bernard is a nice guy to work with. What are you doing here?"

"I came with friends. I was hoping to drum up some business." One corner of her mouth ticked up in a wry smile. "I'm not doing a very good job of it, am I?" She perused the area. "Beginner's mistake. I'm in the library. I'm not mingling."

"Well, let me help with that. I know that Bernard has bought several local businesses and put them under an umbrella company. He likes to support the local economies where he lives. It's good public relations. You might be able to convince him to use your company for that subsidiary. He likes to keep those business interests separate from his hedge fund. I can put in a good word for you if you like."

"Oh my." Her eyes widened. "Would you? That would be quite a feat to sign Bernard's company, even if it's only one of his small companies. It would definitely solidify my position if not get me a promotion." She shifted her weight.

"What's wrong?"

She slanted him a glance. "What's the catch?"

Jack snorted. "And Emma says *I* don't trust anyone. She needs to get to know you." He shook his head. "There's no catch. You're doing me a favor. I'm paying it back. That's how relationships work."

"Not *quid pro quo*."

"Well, to be pedantic, it is *quid pro quo*. I'm helping you because you have agreed to help me. I like the work you've done for me so far. I appreciate your discretion. I like the fact that you are loyal to Mark and Marilyn and are helping them. I think you're good at what you do and I want to help you out. But not in the sense that you are thinking. No sexual favors expected or required. Definitely not in that sense." He tucked a strand of hair behind her ear. "I will tell you that I find you very attractive. And in the interest of full disclosure, I also need to tell you that I'm not a stick-around kind of guy."

"Well, I don't date clients." She glanced away. "I'm sorry. I overreacted. I guess I'm just a little on edge."

"Don't give it another thought. Come on. Let's go find Bernard. He was on the patio a little while ago."

They left the library. Jack greeted several people as they passed through the living room on the way to the outside space. Jack waved to Bernard, who broke away from the group he was talking to.

"Jack! Good to see you, my friend." They shook hands and did a man-hug.

"It's been too long, Bernard." He gestured to Ava. "Let me introduce you to a friend of mine. This is Ava Morrison. She's with Penmans, an accounting firm out of Atlanta."

"It's lovely to meet you, Ava. What brings you to the island?"

"Well, I—"

Jack wrapped an arm around her waist and pulled her in close to his side. "I'll take credit for that. Ava's down for a couple of weeks to visit me." He pressed a kiss to the top of her head. "I'm hoping that she'll have enough work on the island to work down here part of the time."

Bernard smiled benevolently. "Well, well, well. I'm glad to see you so happy. You make a lovely couple."

Bernard turned to Ava. "Jack helped me buy this property, you know. He was also a great help in putting me in touch with contractors. I couldn't have done it without him."

Ava smiled politely. "You have a beautiful home, Bernard."

"Thank you. I'm afraid all the credit goes to my wife." He turned to Jack. "We must go golfing soon, and Ava and Jacklyn can join us for lunch afterwards."

"We'd love that," Jack said. "Wouldn't we, darling?"

"Oh, absolutely." Ava smiled with enthusiasm. *Could she make this work?* If she managed to get any of Wallington's business, she could write her ticket. Her mind raced. But what happened when Wallington realized they weren't dating? Her dreams rapidly morphed to an embarrassing nightmare. She focused back on the conversation.

"Good. It's all settled then. I'll have Jacklyn contact you with some dates. If you'll excuse me, I better get back to my hosting duties. I'll see you both soon."

He walked away and Ava turned to Jack. "Why did you do that? Now he thinks we're a couple. How is that going to help me sign him as a client?"

"I wanted him to think we are together. That was the point."

Her voice held a twinge of frustration. "How does that help?"

"Bernard will only do business with people he knows and likes. If you want a shot at signing his company, you need to get to know him. And that seemed like the easiest way to facilitate that. You don't have the time to wine and dine him. Clients appreciate the long sell. But that's not an option for you."

"But it's going to backfire. He'll know you came here with Evelyn, for goodness sake. How are you going to explain that? I'll—I'll look like some sort of homewrecker." She stared up at him with barely concealed fury.

"Evelyn is frequently my plus-one and vice versa. She's an old family friend. No one will think anything of it." He turned her to face the dance floor. "She's dancing with Rob."

Ava watched them. Rob held her tightly as they swayed to a slow song.

"Rob's had the hots for her for a long time. Evelyn and I both noticed when you arrived. And Rob had his eye on Evelyn."

Heat burned her cheeks. "What are you saying? That Rob approached me to make Evelyn jealous?"

"I'm sorry if that hurts your pride, but yes, I think so. I don't think Evelyn's made up her mind about him yet, but she is interested. You only have to watch them together for a few minutes to see the sparks fly. I'll have a quiet word with Rob and tell him I need to leave early. I'll suggest he offer to drive Evelyn home. Trust me. He'll jump at the suggestion. And thank me as well."

She looked at him dubiously. "I'm not sure you're reading Evelyn right. I think she wants you."

Jack shook his head. "Evelyn's persistent but she'll accept the inevitable. I've always made it clear that we are just friends and that is all we will ever be. Everyone has kind of assumed that we would end up together and I think she has gotten caught up in that. When she takes a moment to consider things, she'll realize we don't belong together. I've known Rob for some time. He's a good guy. And they would make a terrific couple. She just needs to give him a chance.

"Now on to more interesting topics. Rutledge Properties buys a table at a Save the Seas fundraiser held every year at the Grand hotel. The nonprofit raises money for environmental education and awareness relating to the oceans. This year they are advocating to get rid of plastic bags and to have people use reusable bags at the grocery store. Single use plastic bags end up in the ocean, and then in the digestive tracts of marine animals. It's a cause Emma cares a lot about. She does a lot of volunteer outreach for the organization. It will be another great opportunity for you to network. Anyway, it's next Friday. Will you go as my date?"

"Oh, thank you. That is a great idea." Ava beamed. "I would love to go."

At that moment, Evelyn looked over at them. An undefinable emotion crossed her face before her features smoothed out to a blank expression. The song ended and Rob escorted her to the bar.

"See? They're fine. Now, will you dance with me?"

Without waiting for her response, he pulled her into his arms. His hand low on her back sent tingles up and down her spine. Enveloped in his warm embrace, the music washed over her and they swayed to the rhythm. Her hands rested on his shoulders. The warmth of his body radiated through his shirt. She inhaled his scent. Musk and man. All his own. He cinched her in a bit tighter and she bumped against his muscular leg. The crowd receded and it was just the two of them. Time stood still as she opened her senses and simply enjoyed the moment. It had been a long time since she had been held this way.

Several songs later, the band ended their piece and announced a break. She was jolted out of her stupor. The couples on the dance floor had slimmed down to just a few. She had no idea how long they had been dancing. Jack bent his head and whispered, "I can't remember the last time I enjoyed a dance so much."

She looked up at him. Dazed. Vulnerable. "Me too," she said quietly.

"Everyone is a little too tipsy by now to do much networking. Are you ready to go? I'll give you a ride home."

She turned her head and realized he was right. "All right. Let me find the Myrtles and tell them I'm leaving."

"Sounds good. You do that and wait for me inside. I'll have a word with Rob and Evelyn and see you in a minute."

Chapter 16

Ava drove south along Victoria Parkway. Traffic was light as she headed out of the downtown area and toward the less populated residential end of the island. In the small business district, stores and restaurants closed early so the proprietors could have a family life. She made good time and soon pulled into her neighborhood. She waved at the security guard in the gatehouse as the barrier lifted.

Parking in her assigned space, she turned off the engine and leaned back in her seat. Butterflies fluttered inside her. A good kind of excitement. She had been unreasonably pleased to see Jack at the party last night. And even more pleased that he wasn't serious about Evelyn. She hadn't felt this kind of attraction in a long time. Spending time with Toby had always been pleasant. They had a lot in common. It had seemed like a sound idea to date him. But Jack. He was in a different category altogether. He was exciting. Dangerous somehow. The butterflies metamorphosed into chunks of lead. He was a client. She didn't date clients for a very good reason. And even if she could, it would be like the class jock dating the nerdy girl. Those things just didn't happen in real life. He wasn't for a woman like her. She needed to reframe her thinking or she was headed for madness and heartbreak. Maybe she should find a nice guy who worked as an actuary. They could have two point five kids and meatloaf every Wednesday for dinner. That was her future. Sensible. Predictable. She heaved a sigh. Dull.

She exercised her frustration by slamming the car door shut. As she approached the entryway, she stopped short. Someone had shattered the large planters on either side of the front door. Pot shards littered the ground. The shredded remains of the six-foot-tall Majesty palms lay in the debris. She whipped her head around but no one was in sight. With a shaking hand, she tested the front door. She said a silent thanks when the lock held. No one had gotten inside. She unlocked the door, slammed it shut behind her, and shot the bolt across. Dropping onto the sofa, she fished her phone out of her purse and hit the button for Security. She wrapped her hands around her knees and rocked while she waited for the officer.

Within ten minutes, there was a knock at the door. "Security. We had a callout to this address."

She squinted through the peephole. A dark-skinned man in his fifties wearing the security uniform surveyed the mess. She opened the door.

"Beaches Security. I'm Senior Officer Brad Mullins, Miss Morrison."

Ava smiled tightly. "Thank you for coming out."

He gestured to the destruction. "I'm sorry for the trouble you've had." Sympathy flashed across his face. "Unfortunately, there isn't much we can do. I'll take photos, talk to your neighbors to see if they saw anything, and log a report." He scrubbed a hand over his jaw. "As you know, unless we find a witness, it's unlikely that we will be able to find any leads. But you might consider putting a small security camera over your front door. You can get ones that are small and discreet." He pointed at a camera in a neighboring entryway. "I checked the logs before I came. I know this isn't the first incident you've had." Warm brown eyes telegraphed compassion. "Have you had any problems with a boyfriend?"

She wiped clammy hands on her pants. "No, I haven't had any relationship issues. I have no idea what's going on, but I appreciate you investigating this. I may well invest in a security camera. The problem though is that we rent this condo out a lot." She chewed on her bottom lip. "I'm not sure how the vacationers will feel about having a camera watching them as they come and go. But that's not your problem. Please let me know if you find anything out."

"I will, of course, Miss Morrison. I'll also have one of our officers do an hourly drive by just to check on you. Lock the door behind me."

"I will. Thank you for your help. Have a nice evening, Officer." Ava closed and locked the door. Leaning back against it, she inhaled a deep slow breath, hoping to slow her racing heart. Suddenly everything just seemed to be too much. Her job. Sheila. Toby. The threats. Jack. Tears rolled down her face.

Chapter 17

Ava eyed the red one-shoulder dress that she had bought at the boutique Charlene had recommended. It would be perfect for the SOS gala. Her entire body tingled with anticipation. She had been on an emotional rollercoaster. The past few days had been amazing. But part of her thought things were too good to be true, and she was waiting for the other shoe to drop. *Stop ruminating. Tonight is going to be great.* Ava carefully applied her makeup, then stepped into the dress and shimmied it over her hips. She ran her hands down to smooth out the gown and smiled. It fit perfectly. Her yoga and spinning classes had paid off. She slipped on her sandals.

A knock sounded on the door. Right on time. She picked up her clutch purse and hurried to answer the door. Jack's gaze traveled up and down her body before he smiled. "You look wonderful."

They drove the short distance to the Grand Hotel in silence. The oceanfront hotel was lit up for the gala. Sparkling white lights encircled the trunks of the palm trees and outlined each frond. An archway adorned with blue flowers, starfish, and seashells led to the entryway. Guests in evening wear stood beneath the elegant gateway and had their picture taken before entering the hotel.

Jack pulled up to valet parking. The attendant

opened the door for Ava, and Jack walked around the car to give him the keys. Jack took Ava's arm and they went into the hotel.

"The gala is in the largest ballroom. It's this way."

They walked through the open double doors into the ballroom.

"Wow. This is incredible," Ava said.

One side of the ballroom had been foreshortened and large aquariums had been set up then surrounded by paneling. The oversized fish tanks held colorful marine fish and various corals.

"Save our Seas worked with the Society for Protection of Marine Life to set up those tanks. After the gala, the tanks will be relocated throughout the hotel. All the fish will have a home. Emma made sure of that."

Circular tables with blue and silver decorations surrounded a dance floor. At one end of the ballroom a band played. On the wall opposite from the aquariums, various tables had been set up with the items for the silent auction. Waiters with glasses of champagne or fancy hors d' oeuvres skillfully wound their way through the throngs of guests.

"There's Emma." Jack gestured across the room. They weaved their way through the crowd toward her and joined her and her date. Matt and his date du jour were talking to Evelyn and Rob at the bar.

"You're late, big brother," Emma teased. "It's lovely to see you again, Ava." She touched Ava's arm and turned her to her date. "Let me introduce you to Stephen Hill. Stephen, you know Jack, of course, and this is Ava."

"It's nice to meet you, Stephen."

Jack greeted Stephen and shook his hand. Emma had been seeing Stephen casually for some time, and he frequently met the younger man at events with Emma.

"We're expecting a large turnout tonight," Emma enthused. She turned to Ava and explained, "Stephen and I have been volunteering with Save our Seas for several years now."

"It's a very worthy cause," Ava commented.

"Yes, but it's a daunting cause too. The amount of plastic that pollutes the ocean is unbelievable, causing immeasurable harm to marine life. We have been working on a campaign to end the use of single-use plastics, such as grocery bags. Our view is that it's better to reduce the use of plastics, and prevent dumping into the ocean, than organizing beach cleanups. Although we do that too."

"Those are fantastic goals. If there is anything I can do to help while I'm here, please let me know."

"I definitely will! I'll send you an invitation to our next beach cleanup. We try to make a difficult project fun." She gestured in the direction of the SOS sign. "We don't mean to belittle the project but it's easier to get volunteers if you make it like a party." She tilted her head. "Oh, listen, the band is starting." Emma grabbed Stephen's hand and dragged him toward the dance floor.

Rob and Evelyn joined them briefly to say hello before they too headed to the dance floor.

"Well, we're the last ones standing." Jack held out his hand. "Will you dance with me?"

She met his gaze and shivered at the heat in his eyes. She put her hand in his. "I'd love to."

Jack led her out onto the dance floor. He held her

close, one hand very low on her back, and they swayed to the melody of the slow song. Ava felt like they were in their own bubble, everyone around them disappearing. They danced through the next two songs, and then Jack led her to the side of the dance floor.

"Let's get a drink."

The ballroom snapped back into focus. "Yes, that would be lovely," she agreed.

Jack signaled to a waiter.

He grabbed two glasses of champagne when the waiter passed by and handed her one. "There's a silent auction after dinner. Every year, Rutledge Properties bids on something and then raffles it off at the company annual picnic." He gestured to the tables lining the walls. There was a variety of items on the tables. "Help me pick out something to bid on."

"Sounds like fun. Let's go see what they have."

"Last year we were the successful bid on a spa package, which Emma had recommended. Let's see what they have this year."

They wandered around the tables, perusing the items in the silent auction. Each table contained elaborate displays of donated items, including autographed memorabilia, artwork, golf gear, and weekends at local Bed & Breakfasts.

"What about those scuba lessons?" she asked. A local charter boat company offered the scuba lessons and added a day cruise. "That would be fun and should appeal to a lot of people in your company."

"Scuba lessons it is." Jack filled out a card next to the display to place the bid and then it was time to sit down for dinner. They went over to the Rutledge table, and were soon joined by Emma, Matt, and their dates.

Conversation was general while they enjoyed several courses, featuring locally sourced seafood and vegetables. During the dinner, a local marine biologist gave a speech about the ocean's ecosystem.

"Ava, how long are you staying on Victoria Island?" Matt asked after the speaker had finished.

"I have one week left before I have to return to my job in Atlanta."

Stephen turned to Ava. "What do you do in Atlanta?"

"I'm an accountant with a medium sized accounting firm there."

"Ava's a very talented accountant. If you know any businesses that need financial services, I can't recommend her enough. She is doing some great work for Rutledge." Jack leaned his hand on the back of her chair. "Let's hear more about the Save our Seas program. What else can Rutledge do to support the cause?"

"Oh, Jack, you are such a good sport." Evelyn leaned across the table exposing a mountain of cleavage.

Rob shifted in his seat, a sullen expression on his face.

"I would be *delighted* to volunteer as a liaison between Rutledge Properties and Save our Seas," Evelyn gushed.

"Oh well." Jack shifted in his chair and sent a sidelong glance at Matt. "I'm not sure that we're big enough to require a liaison, but I appreciate the offer. And with Emma so involved in the charity, I think we are well-represented."

There was an awkward pause, and then Emma

broke the silence. "I bid on a spa day for two at the Grand Hotel. What did you bid on, Matt?"

"I put a bid on the jet skis. Did you see them? They were sweet. Top of the line."

"Well, you would know, wouldn't you," Jack said dryly. "With the amount of time you spend on water sports, the ocean is practically your second home."

Emma turned to Jack. "And what did you bid on?"

"The scuba lessons. Ava and I thought that might go over well as a prize at the company picnic next month."

Emma turned to Matt and whispered, "Ava and I," using air quotes.

He snickered and spooned up the last of the chocolate dessert.

"Will you excuse me a minute, Ava? I need to say hello to some clients. Matt, I want to introduce you to Tom Winters. He owns several rentals on the oceanfront and I've heard he is considering changing property management companies."

"Sure." Matt excused himself from the table.

"Will you excuse me a moment as well? I can see Bernard signaling to me." Rob inclined his head in the direction of Bernard where he was holding court with several men.

"Of course," Ava replied.

Emma waved them away and turned to talk to Stephen.

As Jack got up, Evelyn moved into his seat, adjusting the skirt of her black backless dress as she sat. She was coolly beautiful and not afraid to let anyone know she knew her value. "I'm so glad we have this chance for a little chat and to get to know one another."

Evelyn leaned toward Ava.

"Oh, me too." Ava forced a smile.

"I've known the Rutledges forever."

"Hmmm." Ava murmured a noncommittal response.

"Our families are old friends." Evelyn continued relentlessly. "I went to high school with Emma."

"Oh, well, that's great." Ava racked her brain for an excuse to leave the table. She pointed vaguely in the direction of the band. "I think Rob is trying to catch your attention."

"I'll go find him in a minute. I hope you don't mind that I'm here with Rob."

Ava's head tilted and she gave Evelyn an odd look. "No, of course not. Why would I?"

Well, I kind of stole him from you at the Wallington party. You know, Jack and I have always been pretty close." She pretended embarrassment, as she continued, "In fact, our families have always assumed that Jack and I will end up together. We'd make a great power couple. I know everyone who is anyone and that's important for Jack's business."

"Really?" Ava was dubious. "Then why did you make off with Rob at the Wallingtons? And why are you here with him tonight?"

Evelyn waved her hand dismissively. "Oh, we're just friends," Evelyn smoothed down some beading on her dress.

"Does Rob know that?"

"Of course." Evelyn gave her a hard smile.

Ava abruptly stood. "Will you excuse me? I need to visit the restroom," Ava said.

"Of course. I'm glad we had this little talk. Now I

better go find Rob."

Ava weaved her way through a crowd of tipsy partiers toward the restroom. As she dodged a heavyset man gesticulating wildly with his drink, Jack put an arm around her waist and pulled her in close to his side. "Ava, let me introduce you to George and Marie Rogers. George is the foreman at the medical complex project. And Marie serves on many charitable committees and basically knows everyone important on the island."

"A pleasure, Ava." George, a tall broad-shouldered bald man who could have passed for the cartoon character on the bottle of a cleaning product, smiled at her. He cuffed Jack on the shoulder. "You are very lucky."

His wife, a petite blonde in a timeless black sheath, smiled at Ava.

Ava blushed. "Nice to meet you both."

"How did you and Jack meet?" Marie asked. "Jack can be as elusive as the lesser spotted blue snaggletooth trout."

Jack held up a hand. "Uh, I'm not really sure how I like that comparison. What does that even mean?"

Marie reached up and put her hand on his cheek. "Dear Jack, you are a lovely man, but you do give the ladies a hard time. Now, there is no evading me when I want to ferret out information. The island's gossip train doesn't run on air, you know. How did you meet?"

Jack wrapped his arm around Ava's waist. "We met through friends."

Marie tilted her head. "I think there's more to the story. And I bet it's delicious. Do tell all."

Jack laughed. As the band resumed playing, Jack

responded, "On that note, I think I need a dance with this beautiful lady. If you will excuse us?"

They laughed and waved them off.

Jack turned to Ava and led her to the dance floor. He pulled her into his arms and moved to the beat of the music. He leaned down to her and murmured, "It seemed like you and Evelyn were having quite the conversation."

"Oh, no, not really," Ava demurred.

"Hmmm…" He leaned in and whispered in her ear. "Don't take Evelyn too seriously. She's a nice person and we have all known her forever, but she has a vivid imagination."

"If you say so." Ava accepted the explanation but hated the way the tension drained out of her shoulders at his comments. *I'm in too deep already.*

When the music stopped, Jack kissed her hand.

"Ava, darling!"

Ava turned when she heard her name, and her face lit up. "Charlene! Brendan! I didn't know you were coming to the gala."

Charlene leaned in for an air kiss. Brendan shook hands with Jack.

"You know how it is. We didn't decide until the last minute. You seem like you're having a wonderful time."

"I am."

"So, what can I report to Lilian?"

Ava made a face.

"Charlene, we talked about this. You're making Ava uncomfortable," Brendan cautioned.

Charlene made a dismissive gesture with her hand. "Oh, nonsense. Ava's not embarrassed. Are you, Ava?"

"Can I get you both a drink?" Jack interjected before Ava could reply.

"Now that's a fine idea, Jack. I'll help you." The men wandered off to the bar.

Charlene leaned in close to Ava. "Now, Ava, this is killing me. You know that, right?"

"Yes, sadly, I do."

"If Lillian thinks I have information about you that I didn't share, that would be the end of our friendship. And we've been friends since before you were born."

Ava couldn't hold back a giggle at the thought of her mother ditching her decades-long friendship with Charlene. "Of course I wouldn't want that to happen. But I also know that there is nothing to share at this point. So, your friendship is not in jeopardy."

"Charlene, Ava! How are you enjoying the party?" Jacklyn Wallington asked, her strapless emerald gown framing the giant diamond around her neck.

"Just fine, Jacklyn. My, what a beautiful necklace."

Jacklyn flushed and fingered the bauble. "Just a little something from Bernard. He can be so generous." She leaned in conspiratorially. "He knew he would be in sales mode tonight with some important people from overseas." She gestured to a corner where Bernard was holding court with several men. "This little thing was his advance apology. He knows I hate those boring discussions. Buy. Sell. Invest. Ho hum."

"It really suits you, Mrs. Wallington," Ava said.

"Oh, dear, Mrs. Wallington is my mother-in-law. Please call me Jacklyn. I'm glad I ran into you both. Bernard wants to put a little golf and luncheon party together. Brendan golfs, doesn't he, Charlene?"

"He loves the game," Charlene chuckled, "but the

game doesn't necessarily love him."

Jacklyn threw her hands up in a voila gesture. "That's perfect." She lowered her voice. "Bernard is a sore loser. Anyway, Bernard and I are headed back to New York tomorrow, but we'll be back for the 4th of July weekend. We must get together then."

"We'll look forward to it."

"Absolutely." Ava added.

"Wonderful. Now I better mingle. Talk to you later." Jacklyn wandered off, a cloud of exotic perfume following in her wake.

Jack and Brendan returned with cocktails. "Was that Jacklyn Wallington?"

"And what was that meteor hanging around her neck?" Brendan asked.

Charlene accepted her drink and smiled at her husband. "That was a gorgeous diamond pendant. Why don't you buy your long-suffering wife one of those?"

Brendan kissed the back of her hand. "Because it would not do you justice, my lovely."

Ava giggled. "Nice dodge, Brendan."

"I'm not sure I should let you get away with that, Brendan." Charlene patted his cheek.

"Darling, you only have to say the word and I'll buy you an enormous diamond like that. Of course, I would have to mortgage the house and work until I'm ninety. But anything for you, my sweet," Brendan quipped.

Ava smothered a yawn.

"I think Ava is getting tired," Jack commented. "Are you ready to call it a night?"

"Sure, it's getting late."

"Will you excuse us?"

Charlene waved them off. "Lightweights. Come on, Brendan. Let's dance." She led him to the dance floor.

They walked out of the ballroom hand in hand out to the lobby. Jack gave his ticket to the valet, who left to retrieve his car. When the attendant brought Jack's car around, Jack helped Ava into the passenger seat. He tipped the valet and got in the driver seat. Pulling away neatly, he turned the vehicle south.

Ten minutes later Jack pulled into the space in front of Ava's condo and parked. Leaning across, he pressed his lips to hers in a lingering, panty-melting kiss.

Ava's breath hitched. "Hmm…That's quite a goodnight."

"I can do better. Just wait." His eyes twinkled. "But for now, I'll see you tomorrow."

Chapter 18

Early Monday morning, a thud sounded as a door slammed shut. Footsteps echoed on the tile floor and a woman's giggle emanated from the kitchen. Jack put his pen down. Matt. He wreaked havoc with females of all ages. He leaned back in his chair and stretched. Time for a break and to refresh his morning coffee.

He sauntered into the kitchen. Matt was draped over a bar stool regaling Elsa with his latest adventure. Both Elsa and Matt started when he came into the room.

"Hey, no need to stop your conversation just because I'm here."

Elsa picked up a towel and wiped the kitchen counter. "Good morning, Jack. Matt just arrived. Would you like some fresh coffee?"

"Sure, thanks, Elsa." His eyes twinkled. "And maybe one of your blueberry muffins?"

Elsa grinned. "You got it, boss."

"Hey, me too. I didn't know you had fresh muffins."

Hands on her hips, Elsa waved them out of the room. "Off with the two of you and I'll bring refreshments into the study."

Matt turned to Jack. "I was hoping to have a few minutes of your time this morning."

"Sure. Come on back."

Jack gestured for Matt to precede him into the office. Matt slumped into one of his client chairs, tossing a leg over the side.

Jack frowned. "This isn't your frat house. Have some care with the furniture."

Flashing an unrepentant grin, Matt moved his leg. "You're grumpy. Where is the lovely Ava this morning?"

Jack closed the lid of his laptop. "She had something to do and said she would be a little late. Now, I'm always happy to see you, little brother, but I suspect this isn't a social call."

Elsa called out through the closed door and Matt jumped up and opened it for her. The aroma of freshly brewed coffee and oven-warm muffins wafted into the room.

"Here, Elsa, let me take the tray for you." A grateful smile on her face, Elsa handed the tray loaded with a coffee pot, cups, and baked goods to Matt.

"If you don't need anything else, I'm going out to do the grocery shopping."

"That's fine. We can help ourselves. Thanks, Elsa."

Matt leaned in and gave her a peck on the cheek. "Until I see you again, my sweet."

A flush crept up Elsa's neck and she smoothed her apron. Shaking his head at Matt's flirtatious comment to the housekeeper who was twenty years his senior, Jack poured two cups of coffee and helped himself to a muffin. Taking a large bite, he chewed and swallowed. "These are always so good. And I hope you don't flirt like that with our other employees. Elsa's an old family friend. But if you act like that with anyone else, we could face a hostile work environment lawsuit. That's it, lecture over. What's up, Matt?"

Matt cleared his throat. "To answer your first question, Elsa is the only person I talk that way to. You can rest easy. In the office, I'm boring personified." He swallowed some coffee. "I spoke with Emma last night. We have been wondering what Ava is really doing here. We checked her out online. Exactly what kind of work is she doing for you? Why do you have an outside accountant working on our books? Why not have our usual firm handle it?"

Jack swore. "Have you or Emma mentioned this to anyone?"

"Of course not," Matt retorted sharply.

"Are you sure?"

"Well, I don't think we did," Matt conceded.

Jack rubbed the back of his neck. "I guess I should have been upfront with both you and Emma from the start. You had a right to know and I kept it to myself. I'm sorry."

"What, Jack, you're not a team player? I'm shocked." Matt's retort was flippant but he leaned forward and put his hands on Jack's desk. "Now I'm getting really concerned. Seriously, kept what to yourself?"

"There's been some money missing." He ground his teeth. This was a conversation he never thought he would have to have. Hell, never wanted to have. "Not a lot. It won't affect your and Emma's payouts nor our ability to meet payroll. Or our yearly profitability for that matter. But it's enough to raise red flags. And it's been consistent. I think someone is embezzling from the company. I don't like that we're employing someone that we can't trust. I've asked Ava to audit the accounts. I wanted to keep this quiet so I couldn't use our local accountant. You know how it is. This is a small town. I didn't want our clients to lose confidence in us. Or our competitors to get wind of this."

Matt shook his head. "You can't really believe that anyone at Rutledge Properties would be stealing, can you? Our employees have been with us for years. We pay them fairly and offer generous vacation time. Hell, no one quits and on the few occasions when there is an opening, we get flooded with employment applications."

Jack's brows drew together. "I know. I don't want to believe it. But it's the most likely conclusion. I find it hard to believe that there have been so many math errors. But, as of yet, Ava has not figured out how the theft is occurring. Nor who is doing it."

Matt toyed with his coffee mug. "So, it could still be an accounting error."

"It could. But I think we both know it's not."

Matt's lips tightened in a flat line. "So you have no idea at all who is behind it?"

"Not yet." He slurped some coffee and burned his throat. "But I'm hopeful Ava will have some evidence soon." He put the mug down. "I should have told you both right away. I'll make a point of telling Emma today."

"Is there anything I can do?"

"I don't think so. At this point, it's probably best to wait for the conclusion of Ava's investigation."

"If she finds something, what do you intend to do about it? We've known most of our employees for years."

Jack scowled. "Hell if I know."

Chapter 19

"Marilyn, that color really suits you." Ava pulled out a wrought-iron chair in the breakfast café. Tucked down an alley, the small restaurant's outdoor patio resembled a garden and was covered with both hanging and potted plants. Marilyn smoothed the skirt of her cinnamon-colored halter dress.

"Mark loves this dress." Her cheeks flushed pink. "I'm meeting him later for lunch. How have you been?

"I've been fine." She took a sip of her coffee, grimaced at the bitter taste, and set it down squarely on a coaster. "Well, actually, no, I'm not really fine."

Marilyn covered her mouth with her hand. "Oh, Ava, tell me what's wrong. I should have known something was up. It's not like you to take a spur of the moment vacation."

She smiled wryly. "You know me so well." She ripped open a sugar packet and poured the contents into her drink. "I was passed over for promotion."

Marilyn's expression softened. "Ava, I'm so sorry."

She fidgeted with her napkin. "That's not all. My boss warned me that they will be making job cuts soon. The Board is meeting in two weeks to make the personnel decisions. If I don't prove I can be a rainmaker by signing a big client before then, I'll be let go."

"I don't know what to say. That's terrible, Ava. I know you love your job. And I know how much time you've devoted to it. You have been a very loyal employee." Her voice was laced with anger. "They don't deserve you."

"You're a good friend."

Marilyn pushed her coffee cup aside. "You're a fighter. I know you must have a strategy to deal with this. That's what brought you here, right? This isn't really a vacation, is it?"

Ava's shoulders sagged. "Yes, you're right. I do have a plan. But how good it is, I don't know. I thought I would go to some of the boat show events and see if I could recruit a client. It's a long shot." She half-heartedly shrugged. "But I've got to do something. I ran into friends of my parents at the Marina's fete for the boat show opening. We mingled at the event, but I didn't come up with any leads there. But they did manage to get me an invitation to Bernard Wallington's party."

Marilyn held up a finger. "Bernard—accent on the first syllable—Wallington? The hedge fund manager? *That* Bernard Wallington?"

"Yes, that's the one. He recently purchased a home here. I guess his homes in the Hamptons, Vail, and Santa Barbara weren't enough. It kind of makes sense though. It's probably quicker to fly here from New York than it is to fly to California. Whatever. It was a good opportunity for me. And Jack Rutledge was there. He has agreed to try and grease the wheels for me with Wallington."

"That's got to be the event of the season. Every mover and shaker between New York and Miami must have been there."

"Yup. It was definitely a target rich environment. But the trick will be to recruit a client in such a short time." Her shoulders drooped. "It's a daunting task. I've no idea whether any of the seeds I planted at the party will bear fruit. Or when."

Marilyn reached across the table and put her hand on Ava's arm. "And I've added to your burden by asking you to help Jack Rutledge. I didn't even think how that would impact your job. It won't get you in trouble, will it? As a conflict of interest or something?"

"There isn't any reason they would find out. And there isn't anything I wouldn't do for you. I hope you know that." Acid churned in her stomach. She wished she had her antacid tablets with her. She thought about exactly how angry Maggie and the Board of Directors would be if they heard she was moonlighting. But Marilyn didn't need to hear that helping Jack violated the terms of her employment contract and would get her fired. For sure. Maybe even sued.

"Anyway, there is something I've been meaning to talk to you about."

"Go ahead." Marilyn took a sip of her hot drink.

Ava grew serious and cleared her throat. "Some really strange things have been going on."

"Strange? Like what?"

"I've had some weird text messages telling me to go home. I assumed someone had a wrong number."

Marilyn leaned forward. "What aren't you telling me? Did something else happen? You wouldn't panic over a text message. And the look on your face definitely says, 'freaked out.' "

"There is more," she admitted. "It gets worse. The

other day I found a note in my work bag. It also told me to go home. So that means someone was close enough to me to put the note in my bag."

"That is scary. What are—" Ava held up her hand to interrupt.

"Some pots were broken. But, that's not all. There was a package in my entry way. It was addressed to me, but the return address wasn't legible. I hadn't ordered anything to be sent here and neither had my mom. It smelled and there were flies circling it."

Marilyn wrinkled her nose. "Go on."

"So I called Security. Someone had packaged up dog shit."

A look of horror crossed Marilyn's face. "Oh, gross. That is so disgusting. You have to call the police now, for sure."

Ava threw her hands up. "And tell them what? They'll probably say it's some kids playing a prank."

Marilyn made a choking noise in her throat. "Well, those are pretty sick kids, Ava. Don't they say serial killers start by torturing animals? This is sort of like that."

Ava shook her head. "Come on, now. This isn't a serial killer. And no animal was tortured."

Marilyn threw her hands up. "Well, that makes it okay, then! What if this escalates? You should at least get a report on file with the police."

"Enough." Ava drummed her fingers on the table. "I know you're right. I'll stop by the police station on my way home. I did report it to our neighborhood's security. I had the security officer open the box and get rid of it. They made a report."

Marilyn leaned across the table and put her hand on

Ava's arm. "Ava, promise me. If anything like this happens again, you'll immediately call the police, and then us. Day or night."

Ava shifted back in her seat. "I promise." She shook her head. "I just don't see what anyone is getting out of this. But I'm glad I told you. It's a weight off my shoulders."

Chapter 20

The one-story police station was a modern building, located mid-island. Palm trees dotted around the parking lot swayed with the ocean breeze. The U.S. and Florida flags fluttered with the wind. A lush green carpet of monkey grass surrounded the walkway to the entrance and provided cover for tiny lizards.

Ava parked in the near-empty parking lot. Automatic doors swooshed open as Ava approached. The cool air-conditioning battled the humid outside air. A middle-aged woman sat at a reception desk behind a clear glass partition. Removing her purple half-glasses, she let them dangle on a chain around her neck and smiled at Ava. "How can I help you, miss?"

"Hello, I'm Ava Morrison. I'd like to report some threats." Ava adjusted her purse on her shoulder.

"I'm sorry to hear that." Worry lines creased the receptionist's forehead and she gestured to the row of plastic chairs that were all connected as if to prevent someone from walking off with one. "Have a seat and I'll see if one of our officers can take your report." She picked up her phone and spoke softly.

A few minutes later the door marked "Employees only" swung open and a uniformed officer came out carrying a file folder and brushing crumbs off his shirt. A powdered sugar mustache covered his upper lip. His gaze swept the empty waiting room before settling on

Ava. "I'm Officer Kline. I understand you want to make a police report."

"Yes." She cleared her throat. "I've had some—"

He held up a hand. "Please come with me." He punched a code into the door and opened it. Ava followed him into a large room full of cubicles. The clatter of keyboards mingled with the clanging of file cabinet drawers being slammed shut. Voices murmured in low conversations. Officer Kline wound his way through the jumble of desks until he reached the back of the room. He pointed to a seat next to his desk and settled himself in a creaky black fabric chair facing the computer. A stained coffee mug sat on top of a stack of papers. A photo of the officer and a young woman on a jet ski was clipped to the cubicle wall. He pulled a form out of a stack on his desk.

He clicked his pen. "Name and address, please."

She gave him the biographical data and he wrote it down.

"Janice said you wanted to report a threat?" His tone made her feel as if she was green and had antennas.

She stared longingly at the exit door, then squared her shoulders. "Yes, I would like to report some incidents." She recounted all the events. "I've got the note here." She pulled it out of her bag and handed it to him. "I can give you screen shots of the text messages. Oh, and I can have Beaches Security e-mail you the reports I filed with them."

He pushed one of his business cards across the desk. "My e-mail is on there. When I get it, I'll finish the informational report."

"Thanks." She fiddled with the strap of her purse.

"Uh, what do you mean by informational report?"

The officer tracked a colleague across the room with a box of pastries before turning back to Ava. "You know, an informational report. A form F-100. We keep it on file."

Ava exhaled. "You keep it on file. But what else will you do?"

His chest puffed out. "We have a lot of real crime, you know. This job isn't just about giving directions to lost tourists. We don't have time to investigate petty dramas."

She sagged back in the chair. Just as she thought. A complete waste of time. He didn't believe her. Or maybe he did but he didn't care. At least not until there was a serious injury. She was on her own.

The phone on his desk rang and his eyes ricocheted from the phone to her.

She got his point. "Well, thank you for your time, Officer. I can see myself out."

Chapter 21

Ava's phone sounded the villain's ominous march from a popular science fiction movie. *Maggie.*

She answered. "Hello, Maggie. How are you?" Ava didn't expect an answer. Maggie had never been much for the social niceties, but Ava couldn't let them go.

"I got a call from a Rob Welton. He says he works for Bernard Wallington."

"Oh!" Anticipation surged through Ava.

Could this really be happening? Had he agreed to give her the business? Maybe Jack was being pessimistic when he said Bernard would want to get to know her better before hiring her.

"That's great news. He's a finance manager in one of Mr. Wallington's businesses. I met both him and Mr. Wallington here on Victoria Island."

"Bernard Wallington the hedge fund guru? That Bernard Wallington?"

"Yes, that's him."

"How do you know him?"

"I met him through some friends of mine. I've been making a pitch for some of his business."

"Well. I'm almost speechless. I said sign a big client and he certainly qualifies. Anyway, Welton wanted to review our terms of engagement before they make a decision."

"That's terrific, Maggie. Did he say when they would decide?"

"He was a little vague on the timeline, but I could make an argument to the Board to postpone any personnel decision for a little while longer if we know we are waiting to hear back from Wallington's firm. That would be quite a catch."

"Thank you, Maggie. I would appreciate that."

Maggie cleared her throat. "I heard something else, too. Something disturbing."

Apprehension flooded through her veins at Maggie's tone. "Oh, yes?"

"Welton said you were working for a company on Victoria Island. Rummages? Rutledges? Something like that? A property investment company. He seemed to be under the misapprehension that Rutledges was on our books. He did misunderstand, didn't he? Because I had my assistant do a search and they are definitely not clients."

Shit. Her worst nightmare. Was the law of unintended consequences going to bite her in the ass? The irony. Was her attempt to recruit Wallington to save her job going to get her fired? That darn Evelyn. She must have mentioned to Rob that she saw me at Jack's office. What could she say? Her thoughts raced. "I have no idea why he thought that." Ava forced a small laugh, but it sounded phony even to her. "He was mistaken. I'm seeing the owner of Rutledge Properties socially. And of course, I'm trying to recruit him." Bile rose in her throat at how easy she formulated the lie. She may not have been happy losing out on the promotion, but she still owed her employer honesty. She rummaged in her handbag for her antacid tablets.

Damn it. Where were they?

"Hmm. Well, I'm glad to hear that. I was hoping that you hadn't done anything foolish like play us. We would not think lightly of such a breach of contract. We would take that very seriously indeed." Ava heard her drumming her fingers on the desk. "I can't stress that enough."

"No! Of course I would never do that!" Ava rubbed a sweaty palm on her pants. "Jack Rutledge is a friend. I can't help it if someone got the wrong impression. Anyway, it's wonderful news that Wallington is considering moving his business."

"All right. I expect you to keep me posted on your progress with Wallington."

"Of course."

"When will you be back to work? Your accounts need attention."

Her left eye twitched. "Next week."

"Hmm. See that you are. Goodbye." Maggie hung up and Ava popped the lid off the bottle of tablets.

Chapter 22

Ava threw her pen down in disgust. It had been a disappointing day all around. A crappy few days. After the buzz from dancing with Jack at the gala, he had dropped her home without making a play to come in. And he hadn't been in the office when she arrived this morning. He hadn't called. He hadn't left a note or even a message with Elsa. She didn't know what to think. He seemed to be blowing hot and cold. Was he just about helping her get Bernard's business? Had it all been an act? Had she been so stupid and naïve to think he was interested in her?

She blew out a breath. *Stop with the pity party and concentrate on work.* She was no closer to identifying the financial discrepancies than she was when she started. Whoever was embezzling knew his or her way around accounting in general, and this accounting system in particular. There were no obvious errors that she could identify. She rolled her neck from side to side. *Maybe a break over the weekend will help me see things more clearly.* She was packing up her briefcase when Jack came into the office.

"Leaving so soon?" Jack asked, leaning against the doorframe.

"I'm sorry, I forgot to mention that I have a friend's barbecue this evening."

"Well, as it happens, Mark has invited me as well.

We could go together." He glanced at his watch. "You'll want time to go home and change. If you can wait ten minutes, I'll change and then I can follow you home to drop off your car. I'll drive you from there."

Here we go, again. Now he is blowing warm. "Ah, sure, thanks. That would be nice." Ava's face heated but Jack didn't seem to notice her stammer and excused himself. He hadn't mentioned the Wallington party or the gala, and she hadn't known if she should say anything. Had she read him wrong? Did he dance like that with everyone? The pain in her gut doubled at the thought that he could be using her. Or had he just been keeping her occupied while Rob made a move on Evelyn? Was she just a pawn? He had said Rob was a friend. Was he just doing Rob a favor? Who played with someone's emotions like that? She needed to stop obsessing over him. Resentment mixed with sadness and regret bubbled up within her.

Ava walked over to the big window facing the ocean and watched a flight of brown pelicans fly low in formation over the surface. The coordinated glide of the feathered aviators somehow soothed her. Jack returned in khaki pants and a polo shirt. He held up a bottle of wine. "This is a nice red from the Bordeaux region. It's a particular favorite of Mark's and Marilyn's."

She mustered a smile. No point letting him see her emotions. "That sounds wonderful. I'll lead the way."

He followed her back to her parents' place in The Beaches. She pulled into her assigned parking space and Jack pulled into the guest parking area. As she approached the door, she stopped short. "Bitch" was painted in large black letters on the front door.

She faltered and then froze, staring at the profanity.

Jack pushed her behind him. "An angry ex-boyfriend?"

"No! This is awful." She shivered and rubbed her arms over goosebumps. "Someone did this in broad daylight," she said in a small voice. "This was not here this morning."

"Wait here." Jack walked up to the door and touched one of the letters. "The paint is dry. Give me the key and I'll check to make sure whoever did this didn't get inside."

"Thanks, I'd appreciate it." She handed him her key. "Jack, wait!" She grabbed his arm and her nails dug into his forearm. "They could still be in there."

His hand covered hers. "I think they're long gone, but I'll be careful. Stay here."

Jack put the key in the lock and threw open the door. "Police!" His shout echoed in the cavernous great room. He moved down the hallway. Throwing open the main bedroom door, he peered in. Empty. He approached the attached bathroom and flipped on the light. Nothing. He went back into the hallway and checked the second bedroom. "It's empty. I don't think anyone broke in. But check and see if anything is missing. I think whoever did this just wanted to give you a scare."

"Well, it worked. Just give me a minute." Her legs trembled and she sank down onto the sofa. She sucked in air but nothing reached her lungs. Panicked, her chest rose and fell rapidly.

Jack dropped into a squat in front of her. "Hey!" He lifted her chin with a finger. "Take it slow. Breathe in for four and out for four. You're starting to hyperventilate. Everything is okay."

Transfixed, she stared at him with the focus of a single cell amoeba. After a few minutes, her respiration slowed.

"You're doing great. No one broke in." He rubbed his hands up and down her arms. "I'll arrange to have our handyman come tomorrow to repaint your door. Do you want to notify the police?"

Still agitated, she tangled her hands in her hair. "I don't really see any point. I know for a fact that they wouldn't do anything." She let out a bitter laugh. "There are no security cameras in this complex since we all have individual entrances." Her eyes darkened with anger. "They would probably charge me for wasting police time. I'll notify Security in any case, so that they are aware." She paused in her tirade. "I appreciate your offer to have it painted. I really don't want to see it again."

"It's no problem." Jack slanted a glance at her. "I couldn't help but notice that you were upset the other day after checking your phone. And now this? Do you want to tell me what's going on?"

She frowned before turning her gaze to meet his. "I was hoping that I had covered that up well." She grimaced. "As to what's going on, I really have no idea." She gazed up at him, wide-eyed. "I've had a couple of text messages calling me a bitch or to go home, someone left a package of dog shit at my front door, the planters in the entryway were broken, and now the graffiti on the door. It's so confusing." Her voice broke. "It just doesn't make any sense. I just don't know why this is happening."

Jack's eyes narrowed. "What about your friend who came down for the accounting seminar? Is he angry at you?"

"Toby? No." She shook her head emphatically. "I was really surprised that he turned up. We were friendly, but the relationship had never really taken off. I really can't see him behind any of this."

Jack sat next to her on the sofa and put his hand on hers. "You never know about people—some don't take rejection well."

She blinked. "True. Toby did kind of want us to spend some time together while he is here. But I've worked with Toby for a long time and seen him interact with others at the office. I just don't think it's him. He doesn't give off the weird stalker vibe. And when I asked him about the text messages, he seemed genuinely surprised. I believed him."

"I had to ask." He rubbed his thumb against the back of her hand. "Is there anyone else annoyed with you? Has anything unusual or out of the ordinary happened lately?"

"No, that's just the thing." She scrunched her face in frustration. "I've thought about this endlessly and I just can't think of any reason for anyone to be mad at me."

"This neighborhood has its own security. Can you ask them to keep an eye on your place?"

"I have. They agreed to have a security guard drive by on a regular basis."

Grim but resigned, Jack suggested, "Let's table this for now. If you want to change, we can go on to Mark's barbecue."

"Sure. I won't be but a few minutes. Help yourself to a drink." She gestured toward the liquor cabinet.

"I'm fine, thanks."

Ten minutes later Ava returned, wearing a halter-backed blue maxi dress and wedge sandals. She had taken a few minutes to repair the damage the tears had done to her makeup.

"You look great." Interest glinted in Jack's eyes.

"Thanks," Not meeting his gaze, she turned away and opened the refrigerator. "Uh, I made a fruit salad last night." She winced.

Wow, great conversation opener.

Jack picked up her keys. She grabbed her purse and the covered dish, and they went out to his low-slung cherry-red Italian sports car. She leaned back into the soft leather seat and inhaled the "new car" smell. He got into the driver's side. He pressed the ignition and the car roared to life. Peering over his shoulder, he reversed out of the space.

She glanced at him. "Don't you want to know the address?"

"Don't need it." He turned the steering wheel to navigate a curve. "I sold them the property a few months ago. It's a duplex. They live in one unit and rent out the other. And it's in a great location—only one block from the ocean. It was a fantastic investment for them."

"Oh, I didn't know. I haven't been down to the island since they bought it. I haven't had a chance to see it yet." She thought about the long holiday weekends when she had gone into the office to catch up on work instead of spending it with friends. What else had she missed out on?

Jack turned out of the subdivision and back onto the main road. He gave Ava a quick look. "Are you okay?"

"I'm still a bit rattled."

"Well, let's get your mind off the vandalism."

"I'm all for that." She changed the subject. "It will be good to see Mark and Marilyn. And I haven't seen their children for a year. Kids change so quickly."

"They're definitely a handful. Mark was a hellraiser when I knew him in school. I can see his son following in his footsteps."

Ava smiled. "It's the cosmos having a laugh at him."

A few minutes later Jack slowed, pulled over to the side of the road, and parked outside the duplex. The vibrant blue two-story house had been split into two apartments. Both units had large wraparound porches. The downstairs was filled with patio chairs and children's beach toys. He walked around the car and opened Ava's door.

Marilyn threw open the front door as they approached. She wore a short red dress with a large floral pattern. "Ava, it's great to see you again." She wrapped her arms around Ava in a quick hug. "And, Jack, I'm so glad you could come."

"Marilyn, it's been too long." He leaned down and kissed her cheek. He set the bottle of wine on the kitchen counter.

A blush turned Marilyn's face the color of her crimson dress. "Come in." She bent and picked up a stuffed frog made famous in a children's storybook. "Please excuse the clutter. I'm still working on getting the kids to pick up their stuff."

They walked through the living area. An L-shaped sectional sofa faced a large-screen television. On the floor, miniature green army figurines lay jumbled among pink plastic ponies with long manes. A granite island littered with kids' cups separated the small gourmet kitchen from the living room. They stepped carefully through the trail of toys and opened the sliding glass door which led out to the backyard. Mark flipped a burger on a small gas grill. Beyond the patio, a circular kiddie pool covered the lawn. He handed Jack a bottle of the local "Crow's Nest" beer from the ice bucket.

"Just in time, Jack. I need some adult reinforcements. The kids are driving me crazy."

A small boy and girl wrestled for possession of an inflatable alligator in the shallow pool as water slopped over the side. "Hey, Billy, Amy, what did I say about playing nicely?" Mark shouted.

Jack smirked and twisted the top off his beer bottle. "Family life. You love it." He took a swallow of his beer. "I like the improvements you've made to the property. Opening up the kitchen to the living room will really add value."

"Thanks, Jack—it was a great find. We love living so near to the beach."

Ava and Marilyn came out of the house, carrying a platter of crispy tortilla chips and homemade guacamole. "Ava has been updating me about the vandalism. It's frightening." Marilyn's brows wrinkled.

"What's been happening?" Mark plated the burgers and gestured to the table. "Come on. Let's sit down and you can tell me all about it. We fed the kids earlier to keep the chaos down."

Over a dinner of hamburgers, veggie burgers, coleslaw, fruit salad, and chips, Ava recounted the events. She threw up her hands. "So that's about it. I reported it to the police but they're not going to investigate. They filed an 'information report.' " She used air quotes around the last words.

Mark's brows drew together. "Victoria Island has always been a safe place with a very low crime rate. Sure, now and then vacationers drink too much and do stupid things."

Marilyn slanted him a reproving glance. "Not just tourists, Mark."

"True." He took a swig of his bottled beer. "It's easy to blame people who aren't from here, isn't it? It's the old 'local' versus 'incomers' divide. And there will always be some crime. But no one really worries about anything serious."

"Do you want to spend the night here?" Marilyn leaned over and put a reassuring hand on Ava's arm. "The couch is a sleeper-sofa."

Ava squared her shoulders. "I appreciate that. I really do. But I'll be fine. However, I might wedge a chair under both the front and patio doors. I know it sounds crazy, but I'm sure it will help me sleep better. And, it was only graffiti. The door can be repainted. In truth, there was no real harm done."

"Well, I don't think it sounds silly at all." Marilyn leaned over and gave her a quick hug.

"I can come over in the morning to repaint your door," Mark said.

"Thanks, Mark. Jack has very kindly offered to have his handyman paint the door."

"Oh." Mark threw a side glance at Marilyn. "Well, that's sorted then."

Chapter 23

Jack sat by his pool and drank his coffee while watching the sun come up over the horizon. His phone vibrated. He glanced at the screen and hit the answer button. "Jack Rutledge."

"Mr. Rutledge, this is Deputy Chief Rawlings." The voice had a southern "Old Florida" drawl. "The Chief asked me to give you a call."

"Thanks for getting back to me." He peeked at his watch. "And so early too."

"When the Chief calls me at home late at night, you better believe I'm going to jump on it. I got here early to see what was going on."

"I appreciate that." Jack fiddled with the table mat for his mug. "I wanted to ask you about progress in the incidents relating to Ava Morrison."

"Can I ask what your relationship is with her? I can't just give out information to anyone. We have privacy laws, you know." He gave a low chuckle.

Jack cleared his throat. "Ava is both a friend and a consultant to Rutledge Properties."

Rawlings chuckled. "I understand. A 'special friend,' huh?"

"No." Jack threw the mat down. "A friend. And a consultant. I don't want to hear any gossip saying otherwise or I would have to reconsider Rutledge Properties' contributions to the VI law enforcement charity fund."

Rawlings chuckled. "You can certainly count on my discretion. We men must stick together. I wouldn't want any woman-trouble any more than you do."

Jack winced at the undisguised misogyny. "Where does the investigation stand?"

"My boys are on top of this. No need to worry, Jack."

"What do you mean by that? Can you tell me specifically what has been done in the investigation?"

"Of course, of course. I wouldn't normally share operational details with just anyone, you understand. But you have been a great friend to law enforcement."

Jack waited. Rawlings cleared his throat. "One of my best boys is going to go out to check out the 'scene of the crime' and give Ava some advice about security."

"So, no actual investigation is going on, is that right? You're just going to do what? Tell Ava to lock her doors?"

"Now, Jack." Rawlings' attitude became less jocular. "We're doing everything we can to investigate these little incidents. But you have to consider that we have real crimes to deal with."

"Stalking is a real crime. And it seems to me that these incidents are escalating in both frequency and severity." *No point in continuing this conversation. This is a total waste of time. I think he's reached the end of his intellectual tether.* "I appreciate your time. Please keep me updated on any progress in the investigation." Jack disconnected.

Chapter 24

Ava woke to a knock on the door. She rolled over and almost fell off the sofa. She threw her arm out to brace herself. Sitting up, she winced at her sore muscles. It had been a bad idea to watch television and fall asleep on the sofa. Yawning, she peered at her cell phone. Five to eight. She groaned. It seemed a lot earlier.

"Just a minute." She hurried into the bathroom and pulled on the fluffy white spa bathrobe that was hanging on a hook on the wall. Squinting through the peephole, she saw an older gray-haired man in a black Rutledge Properties T-shirt and jeans. She undid the chain and opened the door. A red pickup truck with a magnetic sign announcing "Rutledge Properties" on the side was parked next to her car.

"Hello, ma'am. My name is Harry. Sorry to get you up. Jack phoned me and asked me to paint your door."

"Oh, yes! Of course. Thank you for coming out on a Saturday."

"No trouble at all. I just need to take a chip of paint to get a color match. I'll run to the store and get a gallon of paint mixed."

"Thank you, I would appreciate that. Would you like a cup of coffee?"

"Very kind, yes, ma'am. Milk, no sugar, if it

wouldn't be too much trouble." He scraped a flake of paint off the door with a screwdriver.

"I'll put the coffee pot on, and it will be ready by the time you get back."

"Thank you, ma'am." He dropped the paint chip into an envelope.

Ava started to close the door when the raucous outpouring of a finely tuned engine thundered in the quiet neighborhood. *Jack*

Dressed casually in tan cargo shorts and a navy polo shirt, and wearing aviator sunglasses, Jack slid out of the driver's seat. He held a hand out to Harry. "Good morning, Harry. Thanks for coming out so quickly."

"My pleasure, sir." The prominent crinkle lines around Harry's eyes lifted with his smile.

Jack turned to Ava. "Good morning, Ava. How did you sleep?"

She fiddled with the belt of her robe. "Not well, I admit. I know there was no real damage, but the fact that someone was at my home—it just gives me the creepiest sensation. I'm afraid I jumped at the slightest noise."

"That's understandable. I wish you had opted to stay with Marilyn and Mark last night, but I know you didn't want to impose. Harry will get your door fixed. Meanwhile, we need to get your mind off it. Will you let us take you out to breakfast?"

"Us?" Ava's face screwed up and she peeked over his shoulder to see who else was there.

Zeus's furry black head hung out the window of the driver side.

"I hope you don't mind but I've brought Zeus with me." He tipped his head toward his vehicle. "He thinks he's a Formula One driver. He wants to take the car out and check its paces."

Ava's face relaxed. "Come inside while I get dressed. And bring Zeus in. It's too hot in the car for him. I was just going to put some coffee on. You can have a cup while I get dressed.

Jack opened the car door and Zeus flew out. Tail wagging furiously, he ran to Harry, who bent down to greet the dog.

"He likes you," Ava commented.

"Oh yeah. Zeus and I are old buddies. Jack used to bring him around when he inspected the renovations I was working on. I called him the 'junior inspector.' "

Ava led Jack and Zeus into the kitchen and selected a packet of coffee from the cabinet. Jack settled himself on one of the kitchen island high-top chairs and watched her prepare the coffee maker. "Milk? Sugar?"

"Just black, thanks."

She poured in the coffee and water and flicked the on switch. The machine gurgled away.

She handed Jack a mug and put a bowl of water on the floor for Zeus. The black dog slurped noisily. "Help yourself as soon as it's done." Her cheeks warmed and she pulled the edges of her robe closer together. "I— uh—I better get dressed. I'll just be a few minutes."

"Take your time. We're in no hurry." He flipped idly through a magazine before picking up the newspaper. Zeus slurped some more water and then settled down at Jack's feet.

Ava retreated to the bedroom. She pulled a pair of navy shorts and a patterned sleeveless shirt out of the closet. Casual leather sandals finished off her outfit. After running a brush through her long hair and dabbing on some pink lip gloss, she returned to the kitchen. Jack was sipping coffee and glancing through the Victoria Island newspaper. Zeus was curled in a half-moon with his snout on his front paws. The dog's brown eyes tracked Ava's movements.

"Do I have time for a cup of coffee?" Ava asked as she ruffled Zeus's fur.

"Of course. It's Saturday. We're not in any rush. Unless of course you have plans today?"

"No, I hadn't made any plans." Ava topped up his coffee and poured herself a cup.

Jack held up his mug. "You make great coffee."

She tucked a loose strand of hair behind her ear. "I make it New Orleans style. I add chicory to the coffee grounds. It takes some of the bitterness out of the coffee."

"Well, I could get addicted to it." Jack smiled, his eyes sparkling.

Is he flirting with me? This hot and cold is so aggravating. And why do I hope he is? Nothing good can come of it. Only sorrow for me. But I never had these flutters with Toby.

A few short taps and Harry entered. Ava poured an additional mug of coffee, added milk, and handed it to Harry.

"Any trouble matching the paint?" Jack asked.

"No trouble, sir." Harry removed his ball cap, smoothed his hair, and replaced his hat. "I think the paint was bought originally from Victoria Island Paint on Main Street. When I showed them the paint chip, they recognized the color right away. Regent's red. It's one of their signature colors." He took a swallow of coffee. "That's good coffee, ma'am."

Ava beamed.

Jack folded the newspaper and set it on the counter. "Well, good. I'm taking Ava out to breakfast, and we'll let you get on with the painting. Just lock the door when you finish."

"Yes, sir. It will only take a few hours to dry in this hot sun. Be careful not to touch it today, though, Ava, as the paint may be tacky."

"I won't," she promised. "Thank you so much for doing this."

"My pleasure, Ava. I'm only sorry this happened to you."

Jack put his hand on her low back and ushered Ava out. He whistled for Zeus to follow, and they headed for the car.

The door to the neighboring unit opened, and Sadie came out carrying a watering can. Sadie's eye-catching purple house dress was a tad too short and tight.

"Well, hello!" Sadie said, ogling Jack up and down.

Ava flushed. "Oh, sorry! This is Jack Rutledge, a friend of mine."

"It's a pleasure to meet you, Jack." Sadie sent him a flirtatious smile.

Jack blinked in bemusement and shifted his feet as Sadie eyed him like a luxury shopper coveting a couture dress on sale. "Pleased to meet you as well."

Ava smothered a smile. It was funny to see a man as coolly self-confident and unflappable as Jack uncomfortable.

"I saw your door. How upsetting that must have been for you! What an ugly message! What will visitors think when they see that? I'm so glad you're getting it fixed."

Ava gritted her teeth and hoped no one else could hear the sound. "Yes, it was awful. Did you by any chance see anyone near my front door yesterday?"

"Oh, no, dear." She tipped the watering can over her spider plant. "It was the day of my bridge tournament. I was away all day. We play over at the club house. It can be quite competitive." The enthusiasm on Sadie's face made Ava wonder if she played bridge as she claimed or if it was poker. Or maybe they were free and easy with alcoholic beverages.

"Well, I had to ask. It was a long shot."

"What are you doing about the threats, dear?" Sadie turned and poured water over the red geraniums in her window boxes.

"I've notified Security, and they'll make extra patrols around this block."

Sadie's face scrunched with worry. "I'll feel a lot safer knowing Security is out there." She perused the area as if checking if anyone could overhear them. "I didn't want to upset you, dear, but you should know that there has been a lot of talk around the neighborhood."

"What kind of talk?" Ava watched two people jogging down the road. "I haven't heard anything."

Sadie hesitated. "Well, I really shouldn't say."

"It's too late. You can't just bring it up and then not explain."

"Well, some people are saying these incidents are because you haven't had the right sort of tenants."

Ava gaped at her. "Uh…Who exactly are the right sort of tenants?"

"You know…people who belong here."

"Uh, no. I really don't know." Arms on her hips, Ava narrowed her eyes. "Who exactly belongs here?"

Tired of waiting, Zeus seized his moment and bolted after a squirrel. Jack jogged after him.

With a flick of her wrist, she gestured to the dog. "Better go get him, dear. Animals aren't allowed off-leash. The covenants make that very clear." She upended her watering can onto the plant. "Have a good time today."

Just let it go. Take the high road. Even if it's a detour. "Thanks, Sadie. You, too."

Sadie turned away and removed a dead flowerhead. Ava followed Jack to his car.

She fumed as they drove off. "Was she saying what I think she was saying?"

"You mean is she bigoted?" Jack slanted a glance at her. "Certainly seems that way to me."

"Arg. I could scream. She is so offensive." Ava went quiet for a moment. "Do you think what she said about the neighbors was true? I would hate to think that there are more people that think like her here."

"I don't know. I would hope not. It did seem like she was just trying to stir up a little trouble. Come on. Forget about her. You can't control what she thinks or says. Have you ever eaten at the Sea Shack?"

"Nice change of subject. But no, I've never been there."

"Well, you're in for a treat. It's right on the beach. It's a little rustic, but it's an institution. Great food at reasonable prices. Even a few celebrities have eaten there if you believe the rumors."

Chapter 25

The Sea Shack was a dilapidated wooden structure with a faux palm frond roof, open to the air on one side. Photographs of celebrities who had eaten at the decades-old restaurant hung on the wall behind the counter. A long line of eager customers waited to order the breakfast delicacies that the venue was famous for.

Jack and Ava sat outside on picnic-style benches. Jack bit into his sausage and egg biscuit sandwich. Zeus sat at Jack's feet under the table, as if hoping that some table scraps would come his way. "Don't you like your crab Benedict?"

Ava stopped pushing it around on her plate. "It's delicious. You were right about this place." She gestured out to the ocean. "And you can't beat the scenery."

"I'll never get tired of this view. It's why I was determined to build on the ocean front, despite houses being more vulnerable to salt damage. The view is inspiring both on calm days as well as stormy ones. I love to watch when the waves are churning. In the early morning, the sharks feed on small fish in the shallows. Circle of life. I often see dolphins, and occasionally, a right whale on its migration path. It's never boring. Now, you've deflected. I can tell something is bothering you. What is it?"

She laughed. "What isn't it? Sorry, I don't mean to

be flippant. Everything is just getting to me. The vandalism. The stalker. My job." Her fingernails dug into her palms.

Jack leaned forward and put his hand on hers. "Is there anything else I can do? I'll follow up with Bernard's wife. I'll get you another opportunity to make your pitch."

"I'd appreciate that. I'm aiming high trying to sign Bernard. But he seems like my best option at the moment. I haven't had a lot of luck at two different parties." She gazed at her feet for a moment before looking up again. "Client development is hard work. You've been a great help. I really do appreciate it. And you have your own worries."

"It's no bother," he said quietly. "You're becoming very important to me."

Her heart skipped a beat. "I feel—"

"Hey, Jack! Ava! Good morning!" Matt strode out of the restaurant with an order ticket in his hand. "Everyone who is anyone is at the Sea Shack on a Saturday morning."

"Hi, Matt. It's good to see you again."

"Hey, buddy. How's it going?" Matt leaned down and ruffled Zeus's fur. Tail wagging furiously, the dog leaned against Matt and accepted the adulation.

"Sorry to interrupt your breakfast. Jack, I was going to call you to see if you wanted to grab a few beers and watch the game. But clearly, big brother, you have other plans."

"Thanks, Matt. I'll have to take a raincheck. I'll see you in the office Monday. And stop that Cheshire cat grin."

Matt held his hands up in a placating manner. "I'm

delighted for you, Jack. It's about time. We'll all rooting for you, Ava." He winked at Ava. "I'll see you tomorrow, Jack."

Chapter 26

Monday morning Ava pored through the invoices and associated proofs of payment while enjoying the caramel-flavor latte that Elsa had prepared for her. The sugar fix had felt like a necessity this morning. The house was quiet. Jack had an off-site meeting and Elsa was cleaning upstairs. Ninety minutes into her day, she started separating receipts into different piles by vendors. She frowned at the unusually large pile of plumbing receipts. She put them in date order. There was a steady increase in the number of receipts over the past several months. Odd. Either the company had had a serious run of bad luck with the plumbing in their properties, or the receipts were faked to cover false payments. She started compiling a spreadsheet of the receipt numbers and corresponding check payment numbers.

She heard a noise outside and then Elsa opened the front door. Shortly thereafter, footsteps echoed on the tile in the hallway and Jack poked his head in the study door. "Hi," he said with a smile and a twinkle in his bright blue eyes. The expert cut of his dark suit emphasized his broad shoulders. He had added a red power tie. *Darn, he wears that well.*

"Hi, yourself," Ava responded softly but with a smile.

He loosened the knot of his tie. "I'm just going to

change and then I'll be back."

"Fine. I think we have a lot to talk about."

"I agree." Jack shut the door behind him.

While she waited for his return, she totaled the plumbing expenses and printed the spreadsheet.

A few minutes later Jack came back. He was dressed more comfortably in chinos and a black polo shirt with the Rutledge emblem. He pulled a chair over to her desk. "I'm glad you are still here. I was afraid you would have already left for the day."

"I wanted to make sure we had the chance to talk. I've come up with a solid lead on the theft."

"Oh, good." He cleared his throat. "I'm almost afraid to ask. What have you found?"

"There are a significant number of plumbing receipts for Rodney's Plumbing Company. In fact, a disproportionate number in the past six months compared to any previous time. And for fairly large amounts on a consistent basis. Have there been extraordinary plumbing problems or expenses in the last two quarters?"

"Not that I am aware of and if there had been, I would have been told. Rodney's Plumbing is a preferred supplier though. So they would be contracted out for any plumbing issues. I can check with Matt and see if he has had any ongoing problems with the properties we manage. Normally though, for the homeowners that use our property management services, Rodney's invoices the building owners directly. We act as kind of an intermediary. We schedule the work and let the repair men into the property. But unless it's a property that Rutledge owns, we wouldn't get the bill."

"That's what I thought. I've compiled a spreadsheet with the receipts and check payments. Here. What do you think?" She handed him the printed copy. "I would suggest you speak with whomever has oversight over the plumbing repairs and attempt to verify whether the work was actually needed and/or done. I see two possibilities. Either some of the receipts are fraudulent, or there is someone at Rodney's who is collaborating with someone on the inside at Rutledge to create extra work by sabotaging the buildings. Or three possibilities, I guess. You have a lot of buildings suffering plumbing problems at the same time. Possible, but extremely unlikely, I would say."

Jack's features turned stony as he flipped through the multi-page spreadsheet. Finally, he turned back to the first page.

"That is great work, Ava. Leave it with me. I think I know where this is going. While this isn't good news, it is kind of what I was expecting. I'll check this out. But, I'm pretty sure I'll be able to resolve this very soon." He folded the spreadsheet and put it in the top drawer of his desk before locking it.

Chapter 27

Ava stopped at the grocery store on the way home from an evening yoga class. She needed to pick up a few items to restock her refrigerator. Scanning the bag of coffee and the frozen dinner at the self-checkout, she tapped her credit card and bagged her groceries. The automated doors swooshed open and windblown rain slapped her in the face. She clutched the canvas SOS bag Emma had given her to her front and ran to her car at the far end of the parking lot.

She cursed her idea to get extra steps. *Who said sitting all day was dangerous anyway? Catching your death from cold rain can't be much better.* Or slipping on a wet oily pavement. Probably some marketer, hoping to sell—well—she really couldn't think what they would be hoping to sell.

Pressing the remote, she unlocked her car. Ava jumped in, dripping onto the leather seats. She sighed, thinking about the water damage to the interior.

She started the car and exited the parking lot. Pulling slowly out onto the main road, she squinted as the wipers operated in hyperdrive. The monsoon-like rain beating on the windscreen reduced visibility and overwhelmed the drainage areas on the shoulder, pushing the standing water back into the road.

She approached the roundabout slowly, keeping watch for tourists confused by the traffic pattern.

Please, not today. I really don't need to run into someone like that moron last week who reversed around the roundabout because he had missed his exit.

She glanced left to ensure there was nothing coming, then pulled out into the circle. A large vehicle appeared out of nowhere and pulled up so close behind her that she could barely see its headlights.

Idiot. Don't follow so close.

Her fingers gripped the steering wheel so tight they turned white and the tension radiated up her arms and to her neck. She peeked at the speedometer. She was a little below the speed limit. It was a fine balance. Drive slow enough for the road conditions but not too slowly that the truck behind rammed her from behind.

A bright light appeared in her rear-view mirror.

Damn it. Turn off your high beams.

The road widened into two lanes and she pulled into the right lane.

Go on, now. Pass me.

Her eyes ricocheted to her side-view mirror. The black truck pulled into the left lane. Instead of speeding up to overtake, it matched her speed. Water splashed up from its oversize tires and cascaded onto her car.

What a jerk.

All of a sudden, the truck veered into her lane and clipped the front of her car. She slammed on the brakes. Her car tires lost their grip on the road and she spun. Steering was useless. The car veered in its own direction, as if it were floating on water.

What do I do? Think, damn it. Turn with the skid? Or against it?

She turned the wheel in the same direction as the nose of the car.

Too late. The car slid into a one-hundred-eighty-degree turn and was now facing north in the southbound lane. Lights from an oncoming car shone in the distance. She jerked the wheel to the right and drove the car onto the verge. She brought the car to a halt and slammed the hazard warning light button. Hands shaking, she fumbled in her purse for her phone. She had to rest the phone on her leg to tap out the code to unlock it. Without thinking, she scrolled past Marilyn's number and hit the button for Jack.

Jack answered on the first ring. "Hi, Ava. Good to hear from you."

"Hello, Jack."

"Are you okay? You sound odd."

"I'm sorry. I'm sorry." She blinked back tears. "I'm sorry."

"Sorry? About what? What's wrong? Talk to me, Ava."

"I'm sorry for bothering you."

"You will only bother me if you don't tell me what is wrong in the next five seconds," he rumbled.

She swallowed the lump in her throat. "A truck driver pulled too closely in front of me and ran me off the road."

"Are you hurt?"

"No, I'm just scared. What if he comes back?"

"Tell me where you are."

"I'm-I'm on the Parkway just south of the 15th Street roundabout."

"Are you safely off the road?"

"Yes."

"Stay there and I'll pick you up."

"There is really no need. I'll be fine in a few

minutes." Her voice broke. "I guess I just needed to talk to someone."

"Stay there. I'll pick you up. My brother is here with me. He can drive your car. We'll be there in ten minutes."

"All right. Thanks, Jack."

Pull yourself together. You aren't even hurt. Get a backbone, girl.

She clasped her hands together in her lap to stop them trembling.

Headlights grew closer and a car slowed and made a U-turn. It pulled up behind her.

Jack jumped out of his vehicle, came up to her car, and opened the door. He held an umbrella in one hand and pulled her out and put his other arm around her, resting his chin on her head. "I'm so glad you're not hurt. My brother will drive your car. Give me the keys."

Wearing a hooded windbreaker, Matt walked to the front of the car and inspected it. "It's only a damaged fender. Definitely drivable."

"Good." Jack tossed the keys to Matt. He bundled her into his car and put a blanket over her. "Let's get you home and dried off."

"I'll drip all over the leather seat."

"Don't worry; it will dry out." Jack shut the door gently.

He turned to Matt. "Let's go to my house."

"Got it. I'll follow you." He slipped into the driver's seat of Ava's car and moved it back.

Jack pulled back out onto the road. "There's hardly any traffic on the road tonight. You must have been very unlucky."

"Hmm…Or something." She shivered and gathered

the blanket closer around her.

Jack adjusted the heater. "What does that mean?" he asked sharply.

"This may sound paranoid, but it seemed like he was aiming for me."

"Can you describe the truck?"

"Not really." Her brow furrowed. "All I could say is that it was a large black pickup. Visibility wasn't great and I was concentrating on where I was going."

"Any chance you can give a description of the driver?"

"Unfortunately, no." She gulped in air. "Everything happened so fast. I was just worried about keeping my car under control."

"I'll call the police and report the accident when we get you home. Your insurance company will at least want a police report, even if the police can't actually do anything."

"Thanks Jack. I don't have a license plate number, so I don't expect they could do anything. There certainly aren't any traffic cameras along that stretch of road. Thankfully, I'm only shook up. But you're right. Of course the insurance company will want a police report."

"I know it's unlikely that there is any surveillance there. But there is a pinch point near the airport that all traffic on that road has to pass. I'm betting the entry to the airport has some sort of camera. It's probably a safety measure after 9/11. When we get to my house, we need to have a long chat about what has been happening to you. This seems like a whole another level of threat. Things are escalating."

She blinked back tears. "Yes. I think so too."

Jack glanced at her. He picked up her hand and kissed it. "You're safe now. No one is going to hurt you. I won't let anything happen to you."

He slowed down as he approached the turn into his drive. The swoosh of windscreen wipers sounded like a metronome as they rhythmically flicked the driving rain away. He hit the garage door opener and pulled inside. Matt parked her car in the next garage bay.

"Why don't you go inside? I'll be just a minute. I need to have a word with Matt. The door is unlocked." He helped her out of the car and steered her toward the house.

"Okay." Her teeth chattered. She opened the door that led to the kitchen.

Once she was inside, Jack turned to Matt. "Thanks for driving Ava's car."

"Hey, no problem." Matt's eyebrows drew together. "I'm just sorry this happened to her."

Jack explained what Ava had told him about the black truck.

"The police won't do anything even if they found the driver," his brother agreed. Matt pointed to the front driver-side fender. "There's damage here. You can see black paint on the fender."

"Once I get Ava settled, I'll take some photos of the damage for her."

"Let me know if you need anything. I'll head out." Matt tossed Jack Ava's keys and ran out to his SUV.

Jack found Ava sitting on the marble tile floor with her arms around Zeus. He pulled her up. "Come on. Let's get you into a hot shower. I've got some clothes you can wear."

He led her up the stairs to the guest room and into

the bathroom. "Take a shower. I'll have some clothes for you on the bed by the time you come out."

Ava opened the door to the attached bathroom. A giant soaking tub sat under the window so that you could have a view of the ocean while you bathed. The black marble vanity held two matching vessel sinks. She turned the shower on. While she waited for the water to run hot, she tugged on her top. The spandex of the wet sports bra clung to her skin and she wriggled to get it over her head. She peeled the spandex leggings and her underwear down slowly and stepped out of both. Stepping into the Roman-style doorless shower, she adjusted the multiple shower heads, and let the hot water soak into her tense shoulders and neck. She helped herself to the array of luxury bath items hoping that it had been Elsa and not an ex-girlfriend who had selected them.

Finally, she turned the shower off, wrapped herself in the spa-like robe hanging on the back of the door, and opened the bathroom door. A sweatshirt and sweatpants lay on the bed. She held up the sweatshirt. It would come to her mid-thighs. Clearly Jack's. She left off her bra and underwear, which were both soaked. She stepped into the pants, pulling the tie as tight as she could. It gaped at her waist. The sweatshirt was like a dress so she was hoping they were baggy enough that Jack wouldn't notice her lack of undergarments. Once dressed, she went downstairs to the living room to join Jack and Zeus.

Jack sat on the sofa, cradling a large glass of wine. When Ava entered, he gestured for her to sit next to him on the sofa, poured another glass, and handed it to her. "Thank you. I really appreciate you coming to pick me up."

Jack put his hand on Ava's cheek and leaned toward her. "Ava, I'm glad you called me. Stay the night. I have a spare room. I don't like to think of you going home after you were so shaken up."

Ava tilted her cheek into his hand, enjoying the feeling of comfort and safety overwhelming her.

"Thanks, Jack. I don't really want to be alone."

"Here. Just relax." Jack put his arm around her and pulled her close. "Better?"

"Yes, thanks."

She snuggled into him and placed a hand on his chest.

Jack tilted her head up to look at him and leaned down to give her a gentle kiss. The light pressure of his lips sent a bolt of electricity through her body. When Jack deepened the kiss, she wrapped her arms around his neck and snuggled into him. Jack thrust his tongue into her mouth and Ava felt the sensation in the center of her core. He rained wet kisses down her neck and gently pushed her back onto the sofa, covering her with his body. He pulled back, his chest heaving.

"I want you. I've wanted you since the day I met you. But I don't think now is the time for this. You've had a bad scare."

"Jack," she sighed. "I want you too. Don't stop. If there is one thing tonight taught me it's that you have to live in the present. There is never a guarantee of a future."

"I don't need a second invitation." He stood and scooped her up in his arms. He carried her down the hallway, kicking the door to the master bedroom open. He glowered at Zeus who had followed them.

"Out, Zeus." He kicked the door shut and laid her on the bed. He came down on top of her, kissing her hungrily. She savored the moment. The delicious weight of him. Exciting and comfortable at the same time. His hands fumbled with the top of the sweatshirt, trying to pull it over her head.

"Here, let me help." She wriggled up off the bed a little to allow him to get it off.

"Beautiful," he whispered. He pushed her back down on the bed and took one nipple between his teeth. Pleasure shot through her. He pulled the sweatpants down her legs. He kissed her belly and her breath hitched. He created a trail of kisses and moved inch by inch down toward her center.

Jack stood up and Ava grabbed his arm.

"Impatient much?" He laughed. "I'm not going anywhere."

He pulled his polo shirt over his head before unzipping his pants and stepping out of them. He pulled off his briefs and reached into the nightstand drawer and pulled out a condom. He settled back on top of her and slid down until he was kneeling between her legs. He pushed her legs apart and gently teased her with his finger. When Jack removed his hand, she grabbed at him.

"Don't stop, please."

"It's all right, Ava." He laughed. "I'll take care of you."

He bent his head and kissed her. She squirmed under his intimate caress.

"Now, Jack, now." She lifted her hips to give him better access.

"No, but soon, my sweet."

A warm delicious tingling spread through her, promising intense pleasure. The sensation escalated until she reached the pinnacle and exploded. Her muscles quivered and her mind blanked. While she was still recovering, Jack rolled a condom on, moved up her body, and entered her. He filled her.

"Mmm."

"You okay?"

"Oh, absolutely. That feels good."

His back slick with sweat, Jack thrust slowly at first and then with increasing speed. She started a magical climb again. She hit the precipice and let out a cry. Face contorted, Jack followed her over the edge.

He kissed her before rolling off her.

He disappeared into the bathroom for a minute before returning. Climbing back into bed, he pulled her in tight against him, draping an arm over her.

"Feel better?"

She laughed softly. "If by better, you mean amazing, then the answer is yes."

"Well, on that definition, I feel better too." He brushed hair off her face. "I've got a great idea. Why don't we spend tomorrow on my boat? I can take you over to Pony Island. It's a beautiful mostly undeveloped island."

"That sounds lovely. I'll need to go home to get a change of clothes."

He twiddled with strands of her hair. "No problem. We can drive over to your place first thing. You can change and we can grab some breakfast. Elsa hasn't done the grocery shopping yet. Uh, you do have food, right?

"Yes, silly. That sounds like a plan." Ava drifted off to sleep, a contented smile on her face.

Chapter 28

"If you put some coffee on, I'll make breakfast. "How about scrambled eggs and bacon?" Jack asked.

"I just want a quick shower first."

"Sounds good. Take your time. I know where the coffee is. And I can get breakfast started."

He dropped a quick kiss on the top of her head.

While Ava went into the bathroom, Jack went into the kitchen and started the coffee. He rummaged in the refrigerator and found the egg carton and a rasher of bacon. He was cracking the eggs into a bowl to scramble them when he heard a pounding at the front door. The shower was still running so he put the bowl aside and went to answer the door.

He squinted through the peep hole in the door. *Damn it. That guy again. Can't he take a hint?* He opened the door.

Toby blinked twice. "What the hell? Rutledge, right? What are you doing here? Where's Ava?"

Before Jack could answer, Ava hurried to the door, tying the belt of her robe. "Toby! Why are you here?"

He grabbed her by the shoulders and kissed her on the cheek. He gently pushed her aside and entered. "I've been thinking about our talk last week. I know you've been through a shock. Not getting that promotion has really thrown you for a loop and I was not as supportive as I should have been."

"No, Toby, it's fine. I'm not in shock. In fact, I haven't thought about the promotion in days. I'm focused on the future."

Toby gestured at Jack. "You're not yourself. You're acting out of character. Come home to Atlanta and I'll forgive you."

Blood boiling, Ava sputtered, "Forgive me? What the hell?"

What a jerk.

"Forgive me for what? I haven't done anything wrong. And I certainly don't need any forgiveness from you."

Toby continued as if she had not spoken. "When you get back to Atlanta, everything will be the same again. You and I are good together. We make a great couple and I really think that Penmans would be lucky to have us both. Together we can go great places."

Ava was speechless. *What planet was he on?*

She turned to Jack. "Listen, Jack, could you give us a moment?"

"Of course. I'll be in the kitchen."

"Thanks."

Ava turned back to Toby and dragged him into the foyer. Privacy wasn't easy in the open floorplan. She hissed, "I told you we were done, and I meant it." She gentled her tone a little. "Toby, it's not that I don't like you; I do. I just don't think we're right together."

"It's him, isn't it? We were fine until he entered the picture."

When did Toby start to sound so petulant? Had he always been that way? Or is it that compared to Jack, Toby loses.

She swallowed the lump in her throat. "No, Toby,

151

the truth is we were never fine. We were just going through the motions. Admit it. I was never your great passion, and you weren't mine."

"We could still have an amazing future together. With your client base and mine, we could create a firm of our own and be very successful. I'm sure a significant number of our clients would follow us if we started our own company."

"No, Toby." She put her hand on his arm. "My mind is made up. I'm sorry you had a wasted trip."

Red crept up his neck. "Fine, I see it now. I don't know why I wasted my time with you. You aren't going anywhere at Penmans. Sheila is a much better bet."

Jack came of the kitchen.

Her stomach roiled as shame overcame her. *Toby just told Jack he was dating me to get ahead. What would he think of her? Would Jack take that as a signal that she was not good enough for him?*

"Get out before I throw you out." Jack's nostrils flared.

"I'm going, I'm going." He held his hands out to ward off Jack. "No need to get bent out of shape." Jack leaned against the wall and crossed his arms over his chest, watching Toby.

Toby yanked the door open and stomped outside. Ava grabbed the door and slammed it shut in his face. Adrenaline rushed through her body and she shook with fury. "Ooh! What a jerk."

Jack came up behind her and wrapped his arms around her. "Hey, don't let him upset you." He rested his head on top of hers.

"I shouldn't, but that was ugly." She rubbed her arms up and down. 'I didn't know Toby had it in him. I have to question my own judgment since I didn't see that coming. I don't know who I'm mad at—Toby or myself? I should have realized how immature he was a long time ago. I feel like such a fool for not realizing he was just after my help with his career."

"You hadn't slept with him?"

"No, somehow we just never got around to it." She made a face. "I think that says it all about the relationship, don't you?"

Jack kissed her ear from behind and then turned her around. "Don't let him bother you. Come on. Let's go have breakfast.

"Jack, wait." A terrible thought occurred to her. "Do you think Toby could have put the graffiti on my front door?" Ava asked. "I never would have thought he could do something like that. I would have said it was out of character for him, but I also never would have predicted how he acted this morning."

"I suppose it is possible. We need to check on his whereabouts. We can't afford to rule him out, although in my view, he didn't really seem the type. He struck me as more passive aggressive."

"I can check with my administrative assistant. She knows all the gossip. She may know where he was then."

"Do that on Monday. But today, let's enjoy us. Try not to worry."

"You're right." Ava kissed Jack and pulled him into the kitchen.

"It's a beautiful sunny day. A perfect day to be on the water. We can take a picnic. We can't tie up on Pony Island as it has restricted access, but you'll get a great view of the wild horses that run on the beach. It will get your mind off things. I'll text Emma and get her to take Zeus for the day."

Ava made sandwiches and added fruit and drinks to a cooler. They headed north past marshy land inhabited by a large number of great egrets. The large white birds gracefully extended their long necks while they fished for their dinner. Azaleas bloomed with pink flowers along the side of the road. The sky was pale blue and devoid of clouds. A fresh breeze swept in off the ocean, bringing with it the smell of salty air. The marina, located just off the main causeway to the island, was a modern block building with industrial sized garage doors. One of the massive doors was open and a large boat was suspended on hoists. Staff and recreational boaters milled around. The smell of gasoline drifted across the water from a boat that was being fueled.

"I called the marina yesterday and asked them to get my boat out of storage and gas it up." Jack pointed to an empty bay. "Right on schedule."

Ava studied him. "Oh? You were sure I would come?"

He flashed her a grin. "No. But I was hoping you would. There it is." He pointed to a speedboat tied up at one of the jetties.

A marina employee in oil-stained blue coveralls and a baseball cap nodded to Jack as they approached. "Almost ready, Mr. Rutledge." He retracted the fuel line.

The medium-sized boat, with an enclosed pilot area, had seats in the rear for four people. The boat rocked as Jack jumped on board. Jack heaved the cooler into the back of the boat and helped Ava step aboard.

Jack untied the boat from the floating jetty. He pulled away slowly, keeping the boat well clear of the other weekend sailors. With a relaxed grip, he steered the boat across the inland waterway out to open water.

Jack pointed to a pod of dolphins leaping out of the water parallel to the boat. "I'm keeping well below the maximum speed," he shouted above the noise of the engine. "There are lots of marine animals in this area. If we're lucky, we might see a manatee." The gentle sea cows inhabited the warm waters near the island during the summer and migrated farther south in the winter.

The wind whipped her hair around her face. She pushed a strand out of her eyes and smiled at the sight of the perpetually happy-looking mammals. They reached open water and Jack eased the throttle open. The boat leaped ahead. He pointed to a neighboring island.

"Do you know the history of Pony Island?"

"A little. It was owned by wealthy industrialists from the north, but now it's mostly a state park. Oh, and it's famous because a celebrity got married there."

"All true." He decreased the throttle. "We have to be careful and not get too close to the island. I wouldn't want to beach the boat. We could be there until the next tide. You would be surprised at the number of weekend sailors who are caught unaware."

"Wild horses!" She bounced on her toes and pointed toward the shore. "How beautiful."

"Yes, I agree." Jack peered over her shoulder at the horses grazing on the long marsh grass.

They drifted a while, and Jack got drinks out of the cooler. "My family used to camp here when we were kids. We loved exploring. We used to pretend we were shipwrecked pirates searching for treasure. Matt and I used to torment Emma with scary stories about the free-range wild pigs. I feel kind of bad about that now. She used to get really frightened."

"That sounds like a lot of fun for kids."

They sat companionably for a long while, enjoying the view and the warm sun.

As the sun fell lower in the sky, Jack engaged the boat's engine and headed back to Victoria Island. Disturbed by the boat's wake, a pelican launched from the water. Its graceful flight ended when it landed with a splat on a mostly submerged pole. She grabbed her phone and snapped a picture of the bird. She turned and took one of Jack at the wheel of the boat. She would have a photo to remember this day when she went back to Atlanta.

A loud boom rumbled from beneath her feet and rocked the boat. Ava screamed. She fell against the side, hitting her shoulder. Pain lanced through her. A second explosion ripped through the boat and smoke billowed up through the floorboards.

"The boat's taking on water," Jack shouted above the noise. He hit the emergency transponder. "The fuel could explode. We've got to get away from the boat." He threw her a life jacket. "Put this on."

She caught the life preserver with one hand. She struggled to get it over her head with her one good arm. Jack put the strap around her waist and fastened it.

The flooring of the boat was hot underneath their feet. Jack put his hands on her face. "Look at me, Ava."

He turned her head toward him. Her eyes were blank.

"Focus, Ava." He shook her. "We need to get off

the boat now!" Jack hollered.

She shuddered "I don't know if I can swim." She started to hyperventilate. "I h-hurt my arm."

"I'll take care of you. All you need to do is float." He grabbed her shoulders and stared into her eyes. "Do you trust me?"

She shivered and her teeth chattered. "Yessss—"

"Good." He pushed her overboard and she plunged into the ocean. Gasping from the shock of the cold water, she panicked and flapped her arms to stay afloat. The life jacket kept her buoyant and her head above the water.

Jack jumped and hit the water with another loud splash. Treading water, he grabbed the back of her life jacket. Scissoring his legs and with one arm wrapped around her, he kicked away from the boat. Breathing hard and fast, he stroked with one arm, battling the lingering wake of the boat.

Another blast. Debris flew over the side and flames engulfed the boat. Jack doubled his efforts to swim away. If they didn't gain some distance, they would be hit by wreckage. He looked around. The open-sided pleasure cruiser that ran tours to Pony Island had slowed its engines. Tourists were hanging over the side and filming the burning boat with their phones.

The captain spoke through a microphone. "Hang on. We'll pick you up."

Jack waved. He aimed in the direction of the boat, one arm under her armpits. *Breathe. Stroke. Kick. Keep her head above water.* He kept repeating the mantra. Making slow progress in the choppy water, his arms grew heavier with each subsequent stroke. The captain threw a rope toward Jack. Jack reached up to grab it but missed.

Damn it.

The water churned around him. A wave broke and he swallowed water. *Breathe. Stroke. Kick.*

"Hang on. I'll try again." The captain pulled the rope back and threw it one more time. Jack caught it. He looped it around Ava and held on. The captain and his assistant pulled them toward the boat. They lowered a rope ladder over the side of the tour boat. A hand reached down and pulled Ava up. Jack clung to the bottom of the ladder while Ava was pulled on board. Jack tried to pull himself up the ladder but fell back. The captain grabbed one arm and his assistant grabbed his other. They pulled and he toppled over the edge, falling onto the bottom of the boat, exhausted. Loud cheers rang out.

The captain tossed them a blanket. Jack sat next to Ava and wrapped the blanket around them both.

He knelt next to them. "I've radioed the Coast Guard. They should be here soon. In the meantime, are you hurt? We have a first aid kit. But I'm afraid it's pretty basic. It's mostly to deal with sunburned tourists."

"I'm fine, but Ava hurt her shoulder." Jack gulped in air. "I doubt there is anything in your medical kit though to help her." Ava lay curled in a ball on her side. Jack reached out and picked up her hand.

The captain, a man in his sixties with a well-trimmed white beard, and whose ramrod straight bearing suggested a military background, turned on the microphone to address the tourists. "Sorry for the delay, folks. We'll just be here a little longer waiting on the Coast Guard. Then we'll continue to Pony Island."

The tourists shouted out questions. "Did you blow up your boat for insurance reasons?" a middle-aged man in plaid shorts and a pink polo shirt, with zinc sunblock on his nose, shouted to Jack.

"Will you give me an interview so I can post it online?" a young man wearing a T-shirt emblazoned with the local university's mascot asked. "I've got some great video."

"Will I get a refund of my tour price? You're not keeping on schedule. I've got other plans today," a disgruntled man and his wife, both dressed in high-end resort wear, shouted from the back of the boat.

"That's enough, folks. Settle down. Maritime law requires this vessel—like all boats—to come to the aid of those in distress. I'm sorry for the interruption to your tour, folks. But we'll get back on schedule soon." He pointed off the starboard side. "The Coast Guard is almost here."

The tourists pressed forward toward them. The captain waved his arms. "Don't crowd them, folks. They need space."

A faint siren grew louder as the Coast Guard patrol boat sped closer to the scene. The red and white vessel slowed as it approached. The wake of the watercraft gently rocked the tour boat. A second Coast Guard cruiser followed more slowly.

Several Coast Guard personnel in blue uniforms stood on deck. One officer picked up a bullhorn. "We are going to pull alongside. Hold your craft steady."

The captain waved and adjusted the throttle of the engine. "Listen up, folks. The Coast Guard is going to come on board. I need everyone to remain seated."

The university student dangled his phone over the

side of the boat to get an unobstructed view of the approaching vessels.

The Coast Guard officer from the first boat threw a rope to the tour boat. The tour guide caught the mooring line and tied it to a cleat. When the vessels were close enough, he jumped aboard. Another officer tossed a medical box over to him.

The officer knelt next to Ava. His name tag read Benson. Ava stared straight ahead. "Does anything hurt, miss?" When Ava didn't respond, he turned to Jack.

"I think she hit her shoulder. Or her right arm. But other than that, I think she's in shock."

"Got it." The officer turned back to Ava. "Can you tell me your name?"

"Ava." He leaned closer to hear her whispered response. "Ava Morrison."

"Easy now, Ava. I'm just going to take your blood pressure."

He put a blood pressure cuff on her arm and pressed start on the automatic machine. While it inflated, he shone a penlight in her eyes. Once finished, he read the results. "Your blood pressure is a little elevated. But that's normal when you've had a shock. I need to check out your shoulder. I'm going to touch you. Tell me where it hurts."

She nodded listlessly.

He gently prodded her right shoulder and arm. Ava jerked but did not cry out.

"It's probably a strain. I don't think your shoulder is dislocated. You would be in a lot more pain."

Benson turned to Jack. "Now let me examine you."

Jack shook his head. "I'm fine. No need to check mine."

"It's policy. It will only take a minute." Lieutenant Benson put the cuff on Jack. After a minute, he removed it. "Your blood pressure is fine. Now, we're going to transfer you to our boat where we can get you warm and take you to a hospital so you can get checked out."

He pressed the talk button on his radio. "I've checked both. Vitals are good. No immediate danger." He listened to the squawking response through his radio. He turned to the captain. "We think it's too dangerous to do a boat-to-boat transfer with civilians. I have to ask you to take us back to the marina."

The captain held his hand up. "I understand. It won't please some of the tourists. But some of them you can never make happy."

Benson nodded. "If it helps, I can make the announcement."

"Yup. Make it an order. That way we won't have to refund the tickets." He handed the microphone to Benson.

"Attention, folks. My name is Lt. Benson of the U.S. Coast Guard. I'm afraid maritime law requires that we turn this vessel around and take these injured folks back to port. I'm sorry for the inconvenience to your trip and I appreciate your understanding. I know you want them to get medical care as soon as possible."

The tourists broke out in a mixture of grumbling and applause.

The tour boat captain took the microphone back. "All right, the excitement is over. I need everyone to sit down. It's going to get a little choppy as they pull away." When everyone was seated, the Coast Guard patrol boat pulled away slowly, then gained speed.

"I'm going to hook you both up to an ECG while we head back." Benson frowned at the passengers pressing in. "Give us a little privacy, please. If I see anyone filming us giving medical treatment, I'm going to seize your phones."

The tour guide moved to stand at the front, partially obscuring Jack and Ava.

The medic leaned down next to him. "I'm going to hook your girlfriend up to an ECG machine as a precaution. Then I'll do the same for you." He opened a pack of electrodes and placed them on Ava. He connected the wires to the portable machine. She stared into the distance and didn't say anything.

He turned to Jack, holding the electrodes. "How are you?"

"Tired. Cold. Angry. But otherwise, okay."

"Yeah, that all makes sense." He attached the leads to Jack's chest .and scanned the readings. "But the good news is that your ECG is normal. We'll be sending you both to the hospital to get checked out though."

Jack pulled the blanket tighter. "Thanks for that."

The officer pulled out a clipboard and jotted some notes. "One of our maritime accident investigators will meet you at the hospital. They'll want to interview you. Any idea what happened?"

He shook his head. "None at all. I have the boat regularly serviced at the Victoria City Marina, where I dock it. The last service was just a month ago. The blast came from below the floor where Ava was standing. It has—had—an inboard engine. There was the initial blast. We barely got off before the fire started."

"You're very lucky. The boat is in pieces. It's bound to be a fuel leak or an exploding battery.

Hopefully there will be enough debris to identify the cause of the blast. We left the other boat there to pick up debris."

"I hope you can figure it out." His body juddered. "Thank God I trained in rescue swimming. It was too close."

"I'll get you another warm blanket. Hang tight. We'll be there soon."

The boat slowed as they approached the marina. An ambulance, with lights flashing, waited.

Chapter 29

Ava lay in a hospital bed in an exam room in the emergency department. She moved her arm, but the wires connected to a machine that monitored her vital signs restricted her movement. The machine beeped in a constant rhythm. The blood pressure cuff squeezed her arm as it inflated and she winced. A white curtain separated her from the next room where Jack was. An older female doctor, her gray hair cut in a bob, who managed to appear polished and sophisticated despite the stark white lab coat she wore, entered.

"Hello, Ms. Morrison. I'm Dr. Radcliffe. How are you feeling?"

Ava groaned. "I've had better days."

Dr. Radcliffe picked up her chart from the end of the bed. "I'm not surprised. Well, your x-rays don't show any broken bones. No dislocated shoulder. It's just bruised."

"That's good to hear." She sat up and her face contorted. "It hurts like the devil though."

"I imagine it does. I've written a prescription for some pain medicine which you may need for a few days. I'll sign your discharge papers, and the nurse will be in soon to process you out. Any questions?"

"How is Jack? The man who was brought in with me?"

"Are you related?"

"No."

"Well, I shouldn't say, but he's fine as well. You both are local celebrities. Your rescue is all over social media. The hospital has already fielded lots of calls from reporters."

Ava sank back into the bed in relief. "Oh, thank goodness Jack is fine."

"Now if you'll excuse me, I'll go see that your friend is released as well." Dr. Radcliffe stepped out of the cubicle and pulled the white curtain shut behind her. Ava heard her enter the cubicle next door.

"Mr. Rutledge, my name is Dr. Radcliffe. You're a lucky man. Your ECG is normal. I've signed your discharge papers."

"And Ava?"

Dr. Radcliffe laughed. "She asked about you as well. You'll both be able to go home. She's being discharged as we speak."

Jack reached for his clothes. Dr. Radcliffe held up her hand. "At least wait until I leave."

Red creeped up his neck. "Of course."

Dr. Radcliffe shook her head and left. Jack twisted to untie the hospital gown. He pulled on the shorts and shirt that Emma had dropped off.

"It's just me again, Jack." Emma called out. "Are you decent?"

"Depends on the day," he muttered, and more loudly, "Come in."

Emma and a suntanned young man dressed in the U.S. Coast Guard's operational dress uniform of an untucked dark blue buttoned shirt and blue pants tucked into boots came in. "Mr. Rutledge, I'm Officer West. I've been assigned to investigate the explosion on your boat. Is there somewhere we can talk?"

"I've just been discharged. Can you meet me at my house? I'll be in for the rest of the day."

"Of course." He handed his clipboard to Jack. "Write your address. I'll meet you there in an hour. That will give you a little time to get settled in."

"Thanks. I appreciate it."

Chapter 30

On Monday morning, Jack sipped a cup of coffee and winced at the ache in his shoulders.

A perfunctory knock and his office door opened.

"Hello, Jack." Rachel Croft, Jack's administrative assistant, a diminutive woman in her mid-twenties, entered. "I heard about your accident. I'm so glad you weren't hurt."

"I'm fine, Rachel. Come in." Jack eyed the bronzed and glowing Rachel. Born and raised on Victoria Island, she had been friendly with Emma in high school. Emma had recommended her for the job, and she had been with Rutledge Properties for several years.

"Welcome back. How was the Caribbean cruise? I hope you had a good time."

"Thanks, Jack, I did." She set her large bag on her desk and sat down. "But it's nice to be home."

"Great, well there is something we need to talk about."

"Oh? What is that?" Rachel pressed the computer's "on" button.

Jack leaned back in his chair. "We've worked together a long time, haven't we?"

"Yes, of course."

"And have you been happy with your job?"

"Yes, absolutely, very happy." Rachel keyed in her username and password. "Jack, why are you asking me

167

these strange questions?" She pressed her lips into a thin line. "Just a second. I'm having computer problems. Darn thing isn't recognizing my password."

"And it won't. I changed the password. I need to understand why you've been stealing from me." Jack tapped a pen on the desktop.

"What?" She shook her head in denial. "I don't know what you are talking about."

Jack steepled his hands and glared at her. "Yes, Rachel, you do. I found the phony receipts and you were the only person other than myself with the authorization to sign off on the payments. Your boyfriend works at Rodney's Plumbing, doesn't he? It must have been easy for him to dummy up some fake receipts. Then when the invoices were presented for payment, you approved them and paid the bills out of the petty cash fund, and both of you pocketed the proceeds. It was quite a nice set up, but unfortunately, you just weren't smart enough. Just tell me why?"

"Why? You don't have a clue, do you?" Rachel's face twisted. "You have everything. You don't know what it's like to live paycheck to paycheck."

"I pay you a good salary. Was it worth committing grand theft? Risking jail time?"

"You live in this expensive house on the beach and have all the toys." Rachel waved her hands about expansively. "I want that too. You came from the same place I did. You just got lucky. There is no reason you should have all this, and I struggle. And anyway, you won't prosecute—it would make you look stupid. Think how embarrassing it would be for the Rutledge family if people found out that you can't keep track of your own money. That you had it stolen from right under your noses."

"Well, that was a good guess, but as usual you've misjudged me. At first, I had discounted the idea of prosecution, because, as you say, I did not want the negative publicity. But letting you walk away without any attempt at prosecution just didn't sit well with me. I sent copies of all the invoices and cashed checks to the police and gave them a statement. They will be in touch. I've cleared out your desk and will let everyone know why I fired you. Even if you aren't prosecuted, it's a small island, and you will never have a decent job again in this area. I hope it was worth it. Come on. I'll walk you out."

"You're such a bastard," Her face screwed up in fury. "You think you are so smart and that you know everything. Well, I stole money from you for months. Yes, months! And you didn't even notice. And that little accountant you're banging, I bet she screws you in more ways than one."

Rachel laughed at the shock on Jack's face. "What? You think people didn't know about your fuck buddy? Just because I've been on vacation doesn't mean I'm not clued into what is going on around here."

"That's enough." Jack's tone was cold. "I can't believe how wrong I was about you. Well, never mind, it's my mess, and I'm cleaning it up." Jack took her arm and escorted her to his front door. He opened it to two police officers. "Great timing, officers. We're ready here. She's all yours."

"Turn around, ma'am." The gray-haired officer pulled a set of handcuffs off his belt.

Seething, Rachel turned her back and he snapped the cuffs on her.

The younger officer pulled out his Miranda card. "You have the right—"

"Wait a minute, Jack. You don't want to do this!" Rachel protested.

"Yes, I do. Don't act so surprised. I may have chosen not to prosecute for the theft, but I can't forgive the fact that you ran Ava off the road or attempted to murder us when you blew up my boat. You could have seriously hurt or killed us. I can't let that go."

"How did you know?" Rachel's face turned white.

"The black truck was parked on the street in front of your boyfriend's apartment. It was easy to have a police officer drive by to inspect it for damage. No search warrant needed." He peeked at his watch. "The police should be picking up your boyfriend right about now. I'm guessing they'll find evidence to tie him to the sabotage of my boat. The Coast Guard suspect that the ventilation in the battery enclosure on my boat had been sealed to prevent the hydrogen gas from escaping, making it highly explosive. That's attempted murder. You'll be an accessory. You're both going to spend a lot of time in jail. I guess we'll see who cuts a better deal. Do you think your boyfriend is going to take the fall for you?"

The officers escorted her out the door.

Jack watched the officers put Rachel into the police car.

How had things gone so horribly wrong? Had she always been so envious of the Rutledges? How had he missed the signs all these years?

Elsa put a hand on his shoulder. "I'm sorry, Jack. I know you tried to give her a hand when you hired her and helped her to advance her career."

"Thanks, Elsa. Sorry for the drama." He shook his head. "I just can't believe I missed all that anger. She was consumed with rage. How did she keep that emotion so hidden?"

"She fooled us all. I worked with her on a daily basis too, and never saw this coming." Elsa teared up.

Jack put his arm around her shoulder for a moment. "I'm really sorry you had to see that."

"No, it was better that I did. I might not have believed it of her otherwise. I think this calls for chocolate fudge brownies." She squeezed the hand on her shoulder. "I'm going to go make a double batch."

"Thanks, Elsa. I've got some phone calls to make. I don't want Emma and Matt to hear this from anyone else. They knew her arrest was imminent. I told them I would let them know when it was done. I also want to thank the police chief." With heavy steps, Jack walked back to his office. He picked up the phone and called Victoria City's Chief of Police, Ken Davidson. He and Ken served on several charitable boards together. "Ken, it's done. I've fired Rachel and the officers have arrested her."

"Sorry, Jack. I know that was difficult for you," Ken commiserated.

"It was disappointing," Jack admitted. "Anyway, I think that wraps things up. And as for Rachel, apparently Emma was in communication with Rachel while she was away on her vacation. Emma admitted to me that she had unwittingly given her enough information for her to figure that Ava was auditing the books. It was only a matter of time before the thefts were discovered. Rachel had her boyfriend try to scare Ava off so she could continue the embezzlement by running her off the road. I sure hope she never intended to seriously harm Ava. But I'll never really know the truth."

Jack continued, "I've got everything she said on tape."

"That's great. And of course, the paper trail for the embezzlement is clear."

"Thanks, Ken. Appreciate it."

"Always here to help, Jack."

He hit the end button and his desk phone rang. Jack picked up the receiver.

"Mr. Rutledge, this is Harry."

"Hello, Harry. Any news?"

"Yes, sir. I went back to the Victoria Paint Store in town. They confirmed that they mixed the paint. It's their signature color, Regent Red. And what is more, I spoke with the clerk who mixes the paint."

Harry explained what he had learned. Jack thanked him for his work and hung up the phone thoughtfully. Jack made a quick phone call, texted Emma and Matt, and then grabbed his keys and headed out the door to Ava's condo.

Chapter 31

Ava finished wiping the counter and put the cleaning spray under the sink. She surveyed the kitchen and her cleaning efforts with satisfaction.

There was a knock on the door and she opened it to Jack. She smiled broadly and kissed him.

"I thought you were out reviewing a property this morning."

"Something more important came up and I postponed it," Jack replied. "Can I come in?"

"Of course." Her insides twisted.

Was this his way of saying goodbye?

One of the neighborhood's security guards pulled up in his marked vehicle.

Ava turned her gaze from the security guard to Jack. "What's going on?"

Jack squeezed her hand. "Everything is fine."

"Hello, Officer Mullins. Thanks for coming so quickly," Jack greeted the security officer.

"What's happening?" Ava asked. "What am I missing?"

"We've found out the source of your problems. The graffiti on your door, the text messages, the noise complaints…"

"I'll just be a minute." Jack went out the front. He came back a minute later with Sadie.

"Hello, dear." Sadie was dressed in a white tennis

outfit. "I'm happy to help your young man out, but I don't have long. I have a date to play pickleball. I don't want to be late and lose my court. There's always a waiting list, you know." She smoothed the short tennis skirt.

"This won't take long, Sadie. Please, have a seat." He gestured to one of the chairs in the living room.

Sadie sat down.

The officer leaned against the wall and stared at her.

Jack turned to Sadie. "We know that you have been making the noise complaints. And we have evidence that you were responsible for the graffiti on Ava's front door."

Ava gasped. "What the hell?" She gaped at Sadie. "Is that true?"

Sadie stood up and shook her finger at him. "That's absurd, young man. What a crazy accusation! You need to be careful what you say about people. That's defamatory, you know." Sadie headed for the door. "Now, I'm sorry, but I really must go."

"Not so fast. Let's hear what else Mr. Rutledge has to say." Officer Mullins gestured to her to sit back down. His voice rang with quiet authority.

Sadie sat back down abruptly. Jack turned to her. "On the day that Ava's door was painted with graffiti, you asked her what she was doing about the threats. But she never told you about the text messages, did she?" Sadie remained silent. "We also know you bought the paint. We have a clerk at the hardware store that positively identified you as the purchaser."

"What?" Ava whipped her head around. "Are you sure?"

"No doubt about it," he replied. "Come on, Sadie. Tell us the truth."

Sadie threw her hands up. "Yes, it's true. I painted the door, and I made the noise complaints."

"Did you destroy the planters?"

She gave a dismissive wave of her hand. "Again, yes, that was me."

"And the text messages?"

She thrust her chin out. "Yes, those too."

"How did you get my cell phone number?" Ava blinked twice.

Sadie waved her hand disdainfully. "Everything is on the internet these days."

Ava threw her hands up in the air. "But why? What have I ever done to you?"

Sadie's features tightened. "My gentleman friend has been trying to buy a condo near me, but the prices have been too high. I thought if you had problems renting, you would sell it cheaply and in a hurry. Then Dan could pick up a bargain and we could live next to each other." Her knee bounced as she sat. "I'm sorry. I never meant to scare you. I just wanted Dan to live next door. It was just some harmless tricks."

Ava spluttered. "It wasn't—it wasn't just harmless tricks. You ran me off the road! You could have killed me." Her voice rose. She clenched her hands into fists.

Sadie flinched and shook her head. "Ran you off the road? What are you talking about?"

Ava pointed her finger at her. "You ran me off the road in a black truck. That's attempted murder."

Sadie tossed her head. "Don't be ridiculous. I painted your door. I made a few complaints to Security about nonexistent noise. Those I admit." She speared them with an angry glare. "But I never ran you off the road. I don't even have a black truck."

"And what about the dog excrement? That was so disgusting!"

"Gross. I didn't do that!"

Jack gestured at the Security Guard, who turned to Ava. "Ma'am, she's admitted to committing crimes. I can hold her until the police come."

Ava glared at Sadie. "I should press charges. You scared the hell out of me."

"Please, dear, I didn't mean to." Sadie jabbed a finger at her. "You don't live here. I didn't think it really mattered."

"What you did was cruel and selfish." Ava ran her hands through her hair with jerky motions. "How can we possibly live next door to you, knowing that you did these things?"

"I have a proposition," Jack intervened. "Sadie, it's not a tenable situation to have you next door to Ava. I'm sure you can see that. Ava will have no choice but to press charges. If she does, everything you've done will become public knowledge."

Sadie lifted her chin. "I can see where you're headed. I'm in over my head with this property anyway. These condo fees are dragging me down. That crazy management board. They're out of control. It's always easier to spend someone else's money. Did you know they've commissioned a nationally renowned artist to create a sculpture for the entry way? They've chosen a sculpture of a tree! It's a 'neo-Cubist masterpiece.' Just plant a damn tree already. A hell of a lot cheaper. I guess it's time I downsized. I'll go stay with Dan." She grimaced and a flash of irritation crossed her face.

"He's a slob."

A puzzled look on her face, Ava turned to Jack. "But what about the box of excrement?"

Officer Mullins cleared his throat. "Uh, I think I can answer that." Officer Mullins turned to Ava. "I'm sorry to have to tell you that one of our officers was responsible for that."

"What? A security guard? What on earth are you talking about?" Ava's voice rose.

"Chad Thornley. He saw the complaints about your rental. I think he was trying to gain attention. Or maybe make himself important. He's one of our junior officers. He's confessed that he put the box on your porch, and then rushed in to 'save the resident.' I'm afraid I don't really understand his motive."

The blood drained from Ava's face. "That's crazy."

Mullins's ears turned red. "On behalf of Security, I'm sorry for the fright you suffered."

"Thanks. I hope you've fired him."

Mullins glanced around the room before returning to Ava. He cleared his throat again. "Chad is related to the president of the board of the umbrella homeowner's association." He shrugged. "You know how it is." He held up his hand as Ava sputtered. "He's agreed to attend counseling and we're transferring him to the landscaping crew. He has strict orders to stay away from you."

Jack nodded imperceptibly to the security guard.

Officer Mullins's eyes narrowed. "Come on, Sadie. Let's go. Security will be keeping an eye on you until you move out."

She held her hands up as if to surrender. "Don't cuff me, Officer Mullins. I'll go peacefully." Mullins shook his head and followed her out the door.

Ava flopped back on the sofa. Jack closed the door behind Mullins and sat down beside her. He put his arm around Ava and pulled her in close.

Ava stirred restlessly. "I can't believe it. How could someone be so warped? She seemed like a relatively harmless old lady. But in the end, I don't think she had any remorse at all."

"I don't think she is dangerous, but she certainly does seem to be highly narcissistic. She won't harm you anymore. Officer Mullins agreed to supervise her packing a suitcase. She has agreed to stay with her friend Dan until she sells her home. It's her friend that I feel sorry for. Clearly, she has a few screws loose. And so does Chad Thornley, it appears."

"I'm glad she won't be next door. I really don't want to bump into her." Ava hesitated. "So, what about your boat? The boat didn't just explode by itself. And the black truck that ran me off the road? That was just an accident? A road rage incident?"

"Not exactly, no," Jack replied quietly. "I'm afraid those are down to me."

She drew in a sharp breath. "What do you mean?"

Jack rubbed the back of his neck. "Well, my employee was responsible. You discovered the fake billing scheme that was going on with Rodney's Plumbing…"

"Well, yes, they were billing for services never rendered."

He glowered. "It was my administrative assistant Rachel who was involved in the scheme. Her boyfriend Pete worked at the plumbing company, and they devised a scheme to scam money. He would dummy up the fake invoices, and Rachel would ensure the bills got paid without question. I fired her this morning. Anyway, her boyfriend has a black truck. The police identified damage on it that matched the damage on your car. And it's just circumstantial, but Pete was seen down at the marina. He had no reason to be there."

"Oh, Jack, I'm sorry she did that to you. When I discovered the fake billing scheme, I was afraid it was her. She was the most likely suspect since she had access to the accounts." Ava put her hand on his arm. "But I know you thought highly of her."

"My pride took a hit, but I'll get over it. Emma is devastated that someone she recommended did this. I'm just so sorry that you were almost hurt because of her." He wrapped his arms around her, resting his chin on her head.

"Thank you," Ava murmured, her head on his shoulder.

"For what?" Jack responded.

"For solving the mystery. It's such a relief to have it over. And for being you. Most especially for being you."

Jack kissed her on the top of her head. "I care about you." He wrapped his arms around her and held her.

Chapter 32

"I've got to go back to Atlanta tomorrow." Ava didn't meet his gaze.

"I know." Jack clasped her hand. "Let's enjoy tonight. How about I cook us dinner?"

"That sounds lovely." She wrapped her arms around herself.

Our last evening together. I don't want to think about it.

"Red or white?"

"White please." Jack bent over to reach into the wine chiller. He pulled out a bottle.

"How about a Sauvignon Blanc? This one is medium dry."

"Sounds perfect."

Jack poured them two glasses and handed one to Ava.

"What are your plans for the rest of the summer?" Jack asked.

"Well, I've given this a lot of thought. For the short term, I'm going to continue at my job. However, I'm going to write a business and marketing plan for an accounting company. I'm giving some thought to opening my own business. It's early days yet in my planning but I'm sure it's the right decision. I expect the board will vote to let me go, but I should get some sort of severance package. It won't be a lot, but it should help capitalize my business. I would like to sort out as much as I can while I am still employed."

"That's a sound strategy. And will you be coming back to Victoria Island?"

"I'll be back the weekend after next. My family always spends the 4th of July weekend here on the island."

"Will I see you that weekend?"

She released the breath that she had been involuntarily holding. "I would like that very much."

Jack caressed her shoulders. "I very much want to see you again," he said quietly. "You are very special to me." He gave her a slow lingering kiss.

Chapter 33

Ava got out of the elevator, turned right, and headed to her office. Wendy sat at her desk, typing. Her black hair now had pink tips on the end which matched her blouse. A black leather pantsuit and boots completed her outfit.

"I love what you've done to your hair, Wendy."

Wendy flipped her head. "I'm glad you like it. My cousin is in beautician school and wanted to try something different. I was happy for her to experiment on me."

She scrutinized Ava. "You've been back almost a week and you're still relaxed. That must have been some vacation."

Ava laughed. "You have no idea. It was pretty eventful. But I had a wonderful time. Victoria Island is definitely my happy place."

"Well, whatever caused it, boss, it certainly agrees with you," Wendy said. "By the way, Toby has also been by a couple times, but I told him you had a busy day ahead of you with lots of work to catch up on. I didn't think you wanted to see him. If I was wrong, I apologize."

"Thanks, Wendy, I appreciate it. And you weren't wrong. But I probably can't put him off too much longer. I know I need to bite the bullet and just see him. But I'm dreading it." Wendy had never been a fan of

Toby's. Ava only wished she had listened to her.

"Shall I buzz you the next time he stops by?"

"Yes, please. It will also help put a stop to some of the idle speculation about us."

Toby cornered her outside the conference room later that afternoon after a staff meeting and followed her to her office.

"You're a hard lady to find. I hope you haven't been avoiding me."

"Of course not. I've just been busy getting back into the swing of things. I've been away for two weeks and I need to get all my client files up to date. You know how that goes. As soon as you leave, some urgent issue comes up."

"I think we ended things badly," Toby said.

"Well, if by that you mean that *you* acted badly, then yes, I agree. You were completely out of line."

"I apologize. I realize that you were hurt that I was supportive of Sheila, and that your fling was a way to get back at me. I forgive you."

"Wh-What?" She stepped back.

Of all the nerve.

"Toby, it's not all about you."

"Yes, I have been giving our relationship considerable thought." Toby perched on the edge of her desk.

"What relationship? We no longer have one. In fact, I'm not sure that you can call what we had in the past a relationship. We were friends. End of story." She made a chopping motion with her hand.

"I think we should go public with our relationship in the office."

Ava's eyes widened. "Are you kidding me? Have

you heard anything I've said? I'm starting to sound like a broken record."

"I realize that losing out on the promotion has been very upsetting for you, but if we make our relationship known, it will take the focus off your failed career prospects."

Ava pointed a finger at him. "Listen to me carefully." She ground out the words through gritted teeth. "I'm not sure what we had, but whatever it was, it's over. Finished. Fini. Kaput. However you want to say it as long as you get it into your head. I have no desire to see you romantically or at this point even to be friends. Out." She pointed to the door of her office.

"Hormones," Toby muttered. He slammed the door shut behind him.

Ava sat down heavily in her chair.

Finally. Whatever had she been thinking?

The door opened and Wendy poked her head in.

"Is everything all right? You were both a little loud."

"Sure, never better." Ava let out a shaky laugh. "I'm glad that's over. I think he finally got it. I don't think he'll be back. At least, I sure hope not." A flicker of panic appeared on her face. "You don't think anyone else heard us, do you?"

"No, I'm sure no one else heard. It's only because my desk is right outside your door. I'm glad he's gone though. Maggie's administrative assistant messaged me. She's on her way to see you. It would have been bad for Maggie to walk in on that."

"That's the understatement of the year, Wendy." Ava pulled a face. "It's reckoning time."

Wendy's features softened with sympathy. "Good

luck with Maggie. Well, I'm heading out for the evening." Wendy grabbed her purse from her desk drawer and hurried to the elevator.

Maggie passed Wendy in the outer hallway. She stopped short. "My eight-year-old granddaughter has that hairstyle too. I don't like it on her either."

"Good evening, Ms. Ruth, Ava is in her office and expecting you," Wendy said and continued on her way to the elevator.

A red-suited Maggie paused in the open doorway before entering. "Is now a good time to catch up with you? I haven't had a chance to speak with you since you returned from your vacation."

"Of course, Maggie. Please come in." She waved to one of her guest chairs.

Maggie sat down gingerly. Ava wondered if she was afraid the chair was dirty. Maggie leaned back and crossed her legs as if she were attending a tea party. She adjusted the skirt of her designer label suit.

"I've been monitoring your team in your absence. They're performing well on the Midview Hospital account."

"Good. I'm glad to hear that. I've got a great team. They are all individually talented and work well together." Ava forced a smile. She was apprehensive about the discussion even though she was prepared for the outcome.

Maggie put on the half-glasses that hung on a chain around her neck and opened her portfolio. "Now, I've got the agenda for the board meeting here." She held up a piece of paper. Peering over the half-rims, she frowned. "What am I going to tell them, Ava? All week I've been expecting an email from you with the name of an account you signed. It's Thursday at close of business. The board meeting is tomorrow at nine a.m. And I've received no such email. Did you send one?"

"No."

"Did you get a response from Wallington?"

"Unfortunately, when I spoke with Rob Welton this week, Mr. Wallington had not yet made up his mind." *And I may have encouraged him to wait and consider my new firm.*

"I know I told you I could buy you some time. I unofficially sounded out a few of the board members and they were not receptive to a delay. They felt that you had five years to show us that you could be a rainmaker." Maggie whipped off her glasses and skewered her with a piercing stare. "Ava, I take it you did not manage to sign a client?"

"No, Maggie, unfortunately I didn't." Well, not for Penmans. She certainly wasn't going to disclose that.

Maggie jabbed a finger at a file. "Ava, I warned you that the board wouldn't retain you if you didn't have something to show for your two weeks." She waved one hand encompassing the office. "I have to say that I am immensely disappointed in you. I spent a considerable amount of my time mentoring you. You could have gone very far here." She shook her head.

"I do appreciate that, Maggie. I've learned a lot from you over the years. I understand that the board may not retain me. I'm afraid that I'll have to take that chance." Better to let the Board of Directors fire her so that she would get some severance pay. No point sharing her intention to start her own firm.

"Well," Maggie spoke with deep disapproval, "I feel like you misled me. I'm afraid you are not the person I thought you were. I thought you were a team player. I thought you were the right sort of person."

Not that again.

Ava stamped on that thought and pasted a smile on her face. Time to exit with dignity. "Maggie, I will always be grateful for your friendship and leadership. I hope that my hard work and years of dedication is appreciated but I accept that the Board may make a decision that is adverse to me."

"Well, it's settled then." Maggie stood up. She peered at her watch. "It's after hours. I suggest you come in at ten a.m. tomorrow and go straight to Human Resources. I'll share the board decision with you then."

A weight lifted off her shoulders. She contemplated the things in her office, calculating how many personal items she would need to carry out tonight. Not much. "I'll see you then."

"Very well. Until tomorrow." Maggie spun on her heels and walked out.

Ava texted Wendy the news then picked up the empty box that she had taken from the copy room earlier in the week and stored under her desk. She started packing her personal items. She wondered what the severance package would be as she put her diploma in the box. Since it didn't seem like they wanted her to finish the week, she could head to Victoria Island tomorrow afternoon.

Chapter 34

Jack turned into the medical complex construction site and parked in front of the contractor's office. The multi-building project included a hospital, separate medical offices, and several strip malls with restaurants and medical supply stores. When it was finished, it would be a first-rate medical center. Rutledge Properties would make millions of dollars off this deal.

George was flipping through pages on a clipboard.

Jack skirted some building debris and approached his foreman. "Hi, George."

George glanced up and then signed the form and handed the clipboard to the delivery driver. "Jack. I wasn't expecting you today." Rivers of sweat ran down his face and he wiped his forehead with a blue VI fishing tournament bandana. "It's too hot for a tour of the building site today. Come on into the construction trailer and we can have a cold one."

"Lead the way." Jack followed George across the campus. George opened the door to the mobile unit that served as the office and headquarters for the building project. A round wooden table with four chairs ate up most of the space in the room. The wall was lined with metal file cabinets. A small kitchenette had a sink, refrigerator, and microwave. George opened the refrigerator and pulled out two bottles of beer.

Jack shook his head. "Not for me, thanks."

"Suit yourself." Returning the beers, he pulled out bottles of water instead. He threw one to Jack who caught it one-handed. George twisted off the cap and took a long swallow. He pulled out a chair at the table and set the bottle down. "Do you want to go over the schedule for next week? We're on track to make up lost time."

"Not today. There is something else I wanted to talk to you about."

George rocked back in his chair. "Shoot."

"How long have you worked for me?"

George pulled a face. "You know how long. Six months. You recruited me especially for this medical complex construction because I had experience with large projects."

Jack took a swig of water. "And how long have you been stealing from me?

A red flush crept up George's neck. "What the hell, Jack?"

Jack's nostrils flared. "I noticed discrepancies in the accounts and brought in an auditor. It turns out my administrative assistant and her boyfriend were falsifying receipts so she could skim money."

"God, Jack, I'm sorry to hear that. That's terrible." George gave a strangled-sounding laugh. "But why are you accusing me of stealing? You've caught your embezzler. And for fuck's sake, that's an awful accusation. Don't even joke about it."

"I did think Rutledge's money problems were sorted. Rachel and her boyfriend have been implicated in the thefts as well as an attempt to run my auditor off the road."

George spread his hands wide. "There you go,

then. I mean, that's horrible. Rachel has worked for you a long time, but her boyfriend has always been trouble. You know he has a bad reputation. I hope they've been arrested."

"Yes, they have. I will take a hit in the community but I'm putting plans into place to mitigate the reputational damage."

"Good thinking, Jack. If there is anything I can do to help…" George's voice trailed off.

Jack continued to talk as if George had not said anything. "Something has troubled me about the investigation. Rachel's boyfriend was spotted at the marina where I keep my boat shortly before the explosion. But he denies any involvement in the sabotage. And he has friends with a boat there so he could have had a legitimate reason to be there. I believe him. Frankly, I don't think he has the brains to engineer the blast. Road rage is more his style. He's a quick-to-anger kind of guy. He would act impulsively. Rachel was clearly the brains of that team. So it got me thinking who else had access to my boat and would have the knowledge to rig it to blow."

George held up a hand. "Stop right there, Jack. We've been friends a long time. You don't want to say anything that you can't take back."

Jack continued without skipping a beat. "And you came to mind. You can come and go freely at the marina. They know I've let you borrow my boat in the past. And you grew up around boats and would know how to jury-rig them."

"Fuck, Jack." George's face twisted into an angry mask. "Don't say anything else."

Jack's tone turned thoughtful. "The question then

is why. I did some research. Your in-laws' 'cabin' is a luxury home with waterfront access. The property register shows it was bought by you. Your salary would never pay for that house. I walked the construction site last night after everyone left. The contract calls for copper piping. But the pipes you've had installed are plastic. On a building project of this size and with the price difference in the different kinds of pipes, you would have skimmed tens of thousands of dollars. I'm guessing this is not the first project you've shortchanged. You must have thought you had it made when I recruited you for the medical complex. That must have given you quite a laugh. Christmas came early. With the associated medical offices and shops, you stood to steal hundreds of thousands of dollars."

"There's no harm done," George said in a cajoling tone. "I'm just making sure I get my bonus early, that's all."

"The pipes were specified for a reason. The plastic pipes are inferior. Your unauthorized substitution will diminish the quality of the construction and cause problems down the line."

George scowled. "Hell, Jack, I could split the proceeds with you. We can come to an arrangement that benefits us both. There is no reason we can't both be winners from this."

"No, George." Jack's voice was calm but firm.

"Fuck, Jack. You're such a boy scout." George dove for the file cabinet and yanked open the top drawer. He pulled out a gun and pointed it at Jack. His hand shook and the gun wavered up and down. "Shut the fuck up. I'm done taking orders from you."

"Take it easy, George. We're just having a

conversation. Put the gun down."

"You think you're such a hot shot on the island."

"No, no actually I don't. And if I did believe it before, I certainly don't now."

"I gave you a chance. Now we do it my way." George switched the gun into his other hand and wiped his sweaty palm on his pants. "We're going to walk out of here very calmly and get in my truck."

"Just tell me why, George? Don't you think I deserve to know that before you take me to the marsh and dump my body?"

George snorted. "It was easy. Once I skimmed at my first job my wife got a taste of the good life. With the extra money, she's been able to move in all the wealthy social circles on the island."

"That's a pretty damn shallow reason for selling me out. Thank God this is the only project you worked on for me. Put the gun down, George. It's over."

"No, it's not. You're going to commit suicide." He waved the gun around for emphasis. "Poor Jack. The embarrassment of mismanaging your company and letting your assistant steal from you was just too much. You couldn't take the humiliation. So you killed yourself."

Jack shook his head. "I don't think so, George. As a precaution, I sent the Rutledge contract, photographs of the installed pipes, and security camera footage to the Chief of Police. And the Feds are interested in where you've been selling the copper pipes. Apparently, that could fall under racketeering. I don't pretend to understand all the nuances of federal prosecutions but I do know that you don't want to be on the wrong end of a RICO charge. Not to mention what the IRS will have to say about your failure to pay taxes on all that undeclared income. That's the agency I would be afraid of. The FBI can send you to club Fed for a while, but the IRS can destroy you."

George's voice shook. "You don't understand, Jack. I borrowed some money for the lake house from some dangerous people. The interest rate they charge has been crippling me. They just keep adding more and more to the debt. There's no way out. They tell me what to do. How to skim. They ordered me to rig your boat. They are bad people to have as enemies. And they have you and your girlfriend in their sights."

"What about my girlfriend? Why would she be a target?" Jack bit out.

"They didn't want her auditing the books. I'm not sure what they were afraid she would find. All I know is if Marie and I don't do what they say or make a payment, they'll hurt me. Or my family."

"What does Marie have to do?"

"They wanted her to put a scare into Ava. Maybe encourage her to have a little accident."

"Where is Marie now?"

"She's waiting for your girlfriend now in her neighborhood. I'm sorry it's come to this, Jack. Now, enough stalling. It's too late for the both of you. Let's go."

"I'm sorry, George." Jack lifted his polo shirt to reveal the wire strapped to him. "The VI police and the Feds have been very interested in what you have to say. Maybe you can cut a deal if you have information they want." Tires squealed as four police cars with sirens blaring pulled up to the trailer.

Chapter 35

"Miss Morrison, can you hear me?" A pinprick of light shone on her eyelids. She moaned and raised her hand to block out the beam.

"Can you look at me?" a strange voice asked.

"It hurts," she mumbled.

"Ava, it's Jack. You're safe now. The paramedics need to assess your injuries. Can you open your eyes, sweetheart?" Jack stroked her arm.

She blinked. Bright light assaulted her. Her stomach churned. She turned to the side and vomited before flopping on her back.

Gentle hands held her head. "Let's get her in the recovery position." Hands on her back, they rolled her onto her side.

"Miss Morrison. Ava. My name is Charlie." She turned in the direction of the voice and a man in a blue paramedic uniform squatted in front of her. "We're going to take you to the hospital. You may have a concussion."

An involuntary groan escaped her. "Head hurts."

He strapped a blood pressure cuff around her arm. "I know it does. That's why we're going to get you checked out."

"Jack." Her voice was paper thin. She clawed at his arm. "Jack, someone hit me on the head."

"I know, darling. We've got her in custody. She

won't hurt you again." He pressed a kiss to her forehead.

"But why?"

Jack exhaled loudly. "It's a long story. But in short, my construction foreman was cheating me too. The police have both George and Marie in custody."

"How…how did you find me?"

"The police arrested my foreman and he admitted that he had sent his wife after you. He had orders from the criminals he borrowed money from to disrupt the audit. They thought if you were hurt, it would stop any further investigation or at least distract me. He knew about the embezzlement investigation. He was afraid any scrutiny would lead to discovery of his theft. It's my fault. I should have brought Emma and Matt in at the beginning. Emma let something slip to Rachel and George's wife, who both attend an aerobics class with Emma. So your investigation was, if not public knowledge, at least known to the bad guys. And she talked about you coming back this weekend. It's a small community. Everyone knew that you had become important to me. When George said Marie intended to hurt you, I knew you were stopping at your parents' condo before meeting me. So, we rushed here." He motioned at the tall man tapping a cowboy hat against his jeans. Ken Davidson, the chief of police, hovered in the background.

"Thank you," she murmured.

"I'm so sorry this happened, Ava."

"Sir, you can go to the hospital with her and explain everything there. But we really need to get her transported." The paramedic lowered the height of a gurney. He squinted at his partner. "Let's roll her on three. One…two…three." The two medics rolled her onto the stretcher. Releasing the hydraulics, he increased the height and they slid her into the back of the ambulance.

Chapter 36

Dr. Radcliffe shone a penlight in one eye and then the other. "Do you have any blurry vision?"

"No."

The doctor examined the wound on the back of her head. "Ringing in the ears?"

"I don't think so."

"Still nauseous?"

"Yes, a bit. When I move."

Jack rubbed her hand with his thumb.

"Still have a headache?"

"Yes, definitely."

"Can you tell me the months? Starting with December and ending with January?"

Ava recounted the months backwards.

"Good." Dr. Radcliffe pocketed her penlight. "Well, I'm pretty sure you have a concussion. But it appears to be mild. Nevertheless, I'm going to order a CT scan and an MRI." She scribbled something in pen and closed the metal clipboard. She handed it to the nurse. "I've signed orders for the tests." Turning back to Ava, she shook her finger. "If the test results come back normal, I'll release you. You'll probably be here another couple of hours."

"All right. Thank you."

"Now, Ms. Morrison, you need to be a little more careful. I mean this in the nicest possible way. I hope I won't see you back in the emergency room again."

Ava adjusted the hospital gown. "Understood."

Dr Radcliffe turned to Jack. "I'm glad you are both reasonably well. I'm sorry about your boat. And now this."

Jack waved a hand dismissively. "The important thing is that we walked away. Or swam away, I should say. Insurance will cover the rest."

Jack turned to Ava. "About that. The chief sent me a copy of the Coast Guard report."

"Oh, yeah?"

"They weren't able to establish definitively what happened. However, they did recover a piece of the bilge blower and the apertures were blocked. They're speculating that when I ran the blower to vent the hazardous vapors at the marina, something stuck in the hose got sucked up into the blower and obstructed it. So when I ran the bilge blower before departing Pony Island, it failed. Essentially, none of the vapors escaped. And boom."

Ava slumped. "How can they prosecute without a solid conclusion?"

Jack picked up her hand. "It's possible they won't be able to. They've got George on the marina's camera getting on my boat. But proving he sabotaged the bilge blower? That will be very difficult. But they've got him on aggravated assault at a minimum and lots of federal charges. He'll go to jail."

An orderly in white scrubs came in. "I'm here to take you to imaging."

Chapter 37

Jack and Ava relaxed with drinks on the sofa. Zeus lay at their feet. "So, Ava." Jack twirled his wine glass. The silence lengthened.

"You haven't been really happy at your firm in Atlanta. Now that they've let you go, are you going to search for employment with another firm or have you decided to open your own firm?"

"I've pretty much decided to work for myself."

"Can I propose an alternative to those two options?"

She tilted her head. "A third option?"

"Why don't you come work for Rutledge's?"

"Work for Rutledge's?" she croaked nervously, shifting her gaze away from Jack so he didn't see the hurt and embarrassment that would be only too obvious. "You mean work for you? Doing what?" She hoped to delay her response until she sorted out her jumbled thoughts.

"Chief Financial Officer."

"Oh. Chief Financial Officer?" She stiffened and the light went out of her eyes. "Um, I'm not sure what to say."

Jack continued smoothly. "Of course, it's a family firm. It's problematic hiring someone outside the family for a director level position. But I have a plan." Jack picked up her hand.

Ava shifted uneasily. "You do?"

"Yes." Jack got up off the sofa and dropped to one knee.

Ava inhaled sharply.

"Ava, I know we haven't known each other long. But I love you. I think I loved you from the first moment I saw you. You made me trust again. These last few weeks have been the best of my life. My life is now full of joy. Marry me, Ava."

Jack pulled a small ring box out of his pocket. He opened it for her, displaying a large emerald-cut diamond on a platinum band.

"It's beautiful, Jack." Ava teared up. "I love you, too." She smiled through her tears. "The answer is yes!" She threw her arms around him and kissed him. Zeus thought it was a group hug and jumped on them both.

"This gives us another reason to celebrate at our 4th of July party."

Jack's chest eased with a lightness he had not felt for a long time. The future was bright.

Epilogue

Six months later

Ava and Jack lay on teak recliners on their patio. After a day of back-to-back meetings, they had started the evening watching the ocean waves lap up onto the beach. Zeus slumbered peacefully at their feet. Jack picked up the bottle of wine from the chiller and refilled Ava's glass and then his. Elsa's signature charcuterie board sat on the table between their loungers.

Ava's phone pinged. She glanced over at her phone where it lay on the table. She bit her lip. "I bet that's Wendy. She told me she would get back to me today with an answer whether she will accept my offer to come work with me." She picked up the phone with a shaking hand. "I'm almost afraid to read it. I really hope she accepts. I know she was on the fence about moving here."

Jack kissed her hand. "I hope so too. I know that would make you happy. Do you want me to open the message?"

Her mouth suddenly dry, she handed him her phone. "Yes, please."

He opened the text message. "Yes, it's Wendy."

"Well, come on. What does she say? Don't torture me."

"She is accepting the position as your assistant. And even better news—she heard through the grapevine that Maggie was laid off in the latest round of personnel cuts."

"That shouldn't make me happy." She savored her

wine. "But it kind of does."

"Hello!" Emma called out cheerfully, while opening the French doors onto the patio. "Am I interrupting anything?"

"Of course not!" Ava responded.

"There is no 'of course' about it," Emma retorted. "You're in the first year of marriage—still well into the honeymoon phase."

Jack smiled at Ava, brushing his fingers on her cheek, but didn't comment. He turned to Emma. "It's always good to see you, sis. Would you like to join us in a glass of wine? And Elsa has made enough food for a family of four." He pointed to the table.

Emma picked up a piece of cheese from the tray and nibbled on it. "Yum. I can't stay, thanks. I've got an appointment for a haircut. I just thought I would stop in for a minute on the way to the salon." She selected a cracker and munched, brushing crumbs off her blouse. "I just wanted to let you know I heard your old friend Donovan is coming to town. He called me and made an appointment. He's coming into the office tomorrow to view some properties."

"As a matter of fact, I had heard. He called me to tell me he is attending the Navy Seal Charity Dinner at the Grand Hotel. He has decided to take some time off to relax and decide what he wants to do with his future. I think he's thinking of getting out of the military. What's it to you?" Jack asked, with a twinkle in his eye. Emma had long had a crush on his college friend. Emma always found time to "drop in" when Donovan was visiting. Donovan had never made a move on Emma to his knowledge, but Donovan was definitely interested in her.

"Oh. Of course, you knew that," Emma said.

"In fact," Jack continued without missing a beat, "when he asked me to show him some properties that he could use when he had leave, as well as for short term holiday rentals, I suggested that you might be able to help him."

Emma kissed his cheek and hugged him enthusiastically. "You really are the best brother. Thanks for sending him in my direction."

"Well, my work is done here then." Jack winked at Emma. "If you aren't staying for a glass of wine, then hit the road. I need some alone time with my beautiful wife."

"Of course!" Emma chirped happily and flounced out the door.

"What was that about?" Ava asked.

Jack smirked. "When Donovan rang me, he was fishing for information about Emma. I think he is ready to make his move. And I know Emma has always had a crush on him. They would be good for each other."

Ava's smile was full of love, and she leaned forward to kiss him. "You're a closet romantic, Jack. I love you."

"You made me a romantic. I love you too."

A word about the author…

Karen Andover is an author of romantic suspense and contemporary romance. Karen lives an idyllic island life and her goal is to share her happy place with readers one book at a time. She lives in Florida and enjoys spoiling rescue pups. www.karenandover.com

Thank you for purchasing
this publication of The Wild Rose Press, Inc.

For questions or more information
contact us at
info@thewildrosepress.com.

The Wild Rose Press, Inc.
www.thewildrosepress.com